SUDDENLY LOVE

NEW YORK TIMES BESTSELLING AUTHOR

Carly Phillips

Carly Phillips

Do you ever really forget your first love?

Lissa Gardelli hasn't seen Trevor Dane since he left their small town to earn his spot on the right side of the tracks. Ten years have passed but neither has really moved on from their passionate teenage affair or the heartbreak that followed. What starts out as business quickly moves into the bedroom and they discover the sparks between them burn brighter than ever. This reunion can be their second chance, if Trevor can accept everything about Lissa, including her daughter.

* * *

Dear Readers,

Welcome to "Carly Classics", books I wrote earlier in my career that have been modernized for your reading enjoyment. These stories hold a very special place in my heart and I'm thrilled to be able to share them with you now.

All the best,
Carly

ONE

On a mission, Elisabetta Gardelli walked into Consign or Design, a small shop off Main Street in downtown Serendipity known for high-end outfits bought on consignment and unique items created by the owner, April Mancini. The bells rang over Lissa's head as she entered and the yapping bark of a small Yorkshire terrier greeted her.

"Hey, Lucy." Lissa bent down to pet the head of the small dog, whose little tongue licked her, showering her with undying affection.

"Can I help you?" April walked out of the back room. "Oh, Lissa! Long time no see."

Lissa waved a hand and rose to her feet. "I know. Until now I've been able to make do with the clothes in my closet." She hadn't had the extra money to splurge on herself.

April smiled. "That's because you're a good mom and give everything you can to your gorgeous daughter." She tucked her vibrant, layered red hair behind her ear.

At the mention of Olivia, Lissa smiled. It was true she'd rather spend her hard-earned money on her ten-year-old than on herself.

"I still think you should have taken Bradley to the cleaners," April muttered, speaking of Lissa's no-good, cheating ex, whom she'd married right after high school graduation.

"If I could have proven he had access to his family's money, maybe I would have."

Throughout their marriage, it had looked like they had money. The Banks family had all the superficial things covered—a nice house, a Lexus to drive, all the things that looked good to the town. In reality, Brad earned a salary at his father's dealership that paid for the bare bones of what they needed to live, and he'd kept her on a tight budget. Meanwhile, his parents had financed any and all extracurricular activities Brad wanted, including country club membership and expenses.

Lissa had been the stay-at-home wife and mother Bradley had married out of obligation while he'd continued to live a single lifestyle. Even knowing he had affairs, she'd stayed so her daughter could have a stable childhood, two parents living under one roof. But as Olivia grew up, Lissa realized that if the rest of the town was aware of her husband's mistresses, it was only a matter of time until Olivia discovered the same.

Lissa didn't want her baby subjected to gossip, nasty comments, and laughing behind her back at school. Finally, enough was enough and Lissa had walked out.

The good news was, their daughter wanted for nothing. Grandma and Grandpa Banks saw to that. At least Lissa had been smart enough to obtain her online college degree. In between colic, feedings and toddlerhood, a B.A. in journalism had taken her more than five years. When it came to the divorce, she'd received exactly half of what Bradley earned, which had only been enough for her to put a down payment on a house for herself and Olivia. She lived on what she earned. The child support went for her daughter.

These days, she only wanted to reach for the goals she'd shelved when she'd stupidly gotten pregnant as a senior in high school. Though Lissa wouldn't trade Olivia for the world, since her divorce she'd done a one-eighty, determined to teach both herself and her daughter about self-respect.

"Well, I admire you," April said, unaware of the direction of Lissa's thoughts. "You're proof that hard work pays off. I read your interview with Faith Harrington in the *News Journal*. And I'm sure things are looking up for our resident big-time journalist now," April said warmly.

Lissa marveled at the description. She still thought of herself as a small-town coffee-server-slash-obit-writer, not a legitimate newswoman. But ever since Faith Harrington had given Lissa the interview every newsperson on the planet coveted, Lissa had arrived in her chosen field.

"Things are definitely looking up. I've been hired to do a series of interviews for the *News Journal*. Thirty Under Thirty, they're calling it—about men of Fortune 500 companies and entrepreneurs who've made their mark at an impressively young age."

"You go, girl!" April pulled her into a huge congratulatory hug.

Lissa wasn't a warm and fuzzy kind of person, but April was—and in this store, April's rules applied. Lissa allowed the embrace for as long as she was comfortable, then stepped back.

"So what can I do for you?" April asked.

Lissa was supposed to meet her friend Kate Andrews for this shopping expedition, but as usual, Kate hadn't yet arrived. Lissa glanced at the items hanging from hooks on the light green walls. Though Lissa couldn't afford a new couture suit, she knew April would be able to put together the perfect outfit at a reasonable price.

She'd just have to start without Kate. "I need a kick-ass designer suit in order to make a good impression," Lissa said.

"On one of those Fortune 500 guys?" April asked

hopefully.

Lissa drew a deep breath, still unable to believe the subject of her first interview. Just the thought of him set her nerves tingling. "One guy in particular," she murmured.

"Anyone famous I'd know of?" April asked.

Before Lissa could answer, the bells over the door rang again and Kate came bursting through, out of breath. "I'm here. Sorry I'm late, but I'm here." Kate's long hair was in wild disarray, her cheeks flushed pink.

"Let me guess. You overslept?" Lissa laughed, knowing that wasn't the reason.

Kate exhaled long and hard. "I had to stop by my mom's, and she started talking, and I just—"

"—lost track of time," they both said together.

Kate couldn't manage to account for her time and was chronically late, but Lissa could never be mad at her. Kate was one of the good people in this world. They'd both grown up in Serendipity, gone to the same elementary, middle, and high schools—and had never spoken to each other. Oh, they glared plenty, Kate being one of those girls with money, like Faith Harrington. Lissa had been a townie without.

To her shame, Lissa had carried that attitude into the present, at least where Faith was concerned, and she cringed at the memory of how badly she'd treated the other woman when she'd returned to town. Even though Faith's father had been convicted of running a Ponzi scheme that rivaled Bernie Madoff's, Lissa had thought Faith's life had been easy. How wrong she'd been.

Thank goodness Faith had seen through Lissa's bitterness about her own life and given her a chance despite her attitude. Faith had taught Lissa the meaning of generosity and of rising above it all. Lissa was more grateful for that hard lesson than for the actual interview.

April clapped her hands, capturing her attention. "Lissa was just about to tell me why she needed a kick-ass designer suit. And which Fortune 500 guy she wanted to impress." April lifted one perfectly penciled eyebrow.

"Well? Are you going to tell her?" Kate asked. "It's Trevor Dane!" she said, blurting out the news before Lissa could do it herself.

April's eyes opened wide. "Trevor Dane. Your... I mean..."

"My high school sweetheart," Lissa said. The only man she'd ever truly loved and the one she'd hurt beyond reason.

The *News Journal's* list of interviewees was set in stone. She had no choice but to face Trevor again for the first time since telling him she was pregnant with Bradley Banks's baby, ten years before. Although Faith

Harrington had been given a second chance with Ethan Barron, another man Lissa would be interviewing, she already knew she had royally screwed up any shot with Trevor Dane a decade earlier.

She didn't deserve another.

And to put an exclamation point on that old statement, Trevor had gone away to college; he lived in Manhattan; and though he'd visited Serendipity and his family over the years, when it came to Lissa, he'd never looked back.

*   *   *

"*News Journal* magazine wants to interview you," Alexander Wittman, president and CEO of Wittman Financial Management and the son of the firm's founder, said as he walked into Trevor Dane's corner office.

Trevor didn't turn. Instead he stared out at the streets of Manhattan from the luxury high-rise office building on Broad Street, wondering how a kid from the wrong side of the tracks had arrived at this point. Brains, hard work, and a helluva lot of luck. That and a burning desire to get out of his hometown of Serendipity, New York, and rarely go back. It'd be *never* if not for his family, Trevor thought wryly.

"Did you hear me?" Alex asked.

Trevor pivoted to face his boss and mentor. "I was

just taking it in. *News Journal*, huh?" Like *Forbes*, the magazine was a must-read in the business world.

"You're an up-and-comer," the man said proudly.

"Thanks. I owe it to you." A decade older than Trevor, Alex had been his mentor since he'd interned with him one summer. "My secretary gave me a schedule of events the reporter will be attending with me. Apparently she wants to follow me around even in my off hours," he muttered.

She was even supposed to attend the annual charity gala the firm was sponsoring on Friday night at the Waldorf. Though Trevor wasn't pleased, it did save him the hassle of finding a date, the need for which he'd been ignoring.

"The price we pay," Alex said on a laugh. "Maybe she'll be a beauty."

Trevor raised an eyebrow. "I'm not about to get us slapped with a sexual harassment suit by coming on to the reporter."

"You know what your problem is?" Alex asked.

"Wasn't aware I had one." Trevor folded his arms across his chest. "Care to enlighten me?"

"You're all work and no play. You don't want to end up old and alone, not when the alternative is so much better." Alex ran a hand through his thick black hair and eyed Trevor with a knowing look that meant he wouldn't drop the subject easily. The man was always after Trevor to look harder at the women he dated, give them more than a couple of chances before deciding to break things off.

But Alex had married his college sweetheart and hadn't looked at another woman since. Trevor wished he'd been so lucky. Every woman he dated left him cold because no one could live up to the memory of the one who got away—breaking his heart and ruining him for anyone who came after her.

"Give me a break. You like how much money I bring in and that takes up all my time." Trevor walked around his desk and placed a hand on the other man's back. "So it's time for you to let me do my thing before the reporter arrives." In fact, she was due any minute.

"Fine. Subject dropped. For now. But Emma insists you come to dinner Saturday night at our penthouse. She said she won't take no for an answer."

"As long as she's not trying to set me up with one of her friends," Trevor said, accepting. He loved Alex's wife and wouldn't deny her a thing.

"The fact that you're free on such short notice just backs up my point. You need—"

"—to get to work," Trevor said. "Tell Emma I'll see her on Saturday."

Before Alex could depart, a knock sounded on Trevor's office door. "Come in."

His secretary, Collette, opened the door. "Mr. Dane, your nine-thirty appointment is here."

Trevor nodded. "Show her in, please."

"I'll just stay and say hello to the reporter," Alex said, puffing out his chest a bit.

Trevor grinned. The man did love publicity.

"Right this way," Trevor heard Collette say before she stepped back in. "Mr. Dane, Mr. Wittman, this is Ms. Elisabetta Gardelli from the *News Journal*." Collette stepped aside.

And the woman who'd haunted his dreams for the past ten years took his middle-aged secretary's place in the doorway.

"Hello, Mr. Wittman." Elisabetta nodded at Alex. "Hi, Trevor." Her husky voice had only grown deeper, sexier.

He immediately found himself sucked into those green eyes, the color of freshly cut grass. Just the sight of her was a sucker punch to his stomach as memories that still had the power to gut him swept over him like a tsunami. "Oh, no. No fucking way."

Lissa paled at the words that slipped from his mouth.

Alex stepped back, his expression full of stark disbelief. Trevor was sure the man had never heard him speak that way.

"You two obviously know each other," Alex said.

"From high school," Lissa said, her voice . steady anymore. "It's been awhile." She met his gaz. giving him time to adjust to the shock.

He tried to find his composure but surprise made it impossible. Since she blatantly stared at him, he returned the favor. Here in a professional capacity, she wore a simple black dress obviously meant to give her a professional yet elegant appearance, but her body outshone any dress and her cropped jacket showcased her full breasts and indented waist. Time had brought changes to the girl he'd known—and they were good ones.

Curves he'd felt in his hands as a teenager had only blossomed over the years. Glossy hair he'd once wrapped around his fingers fell over her shoulders, while her face had filled out in a way that highlighted her cheekbones and full lips. She was still beautiful. And there was no way he could deal with her on a professional level and remain immune. No way he could let her trail after him for days and go back to his solitary life afterward.

"I can't do this," Trevor said into the uncomfortable silence. He didn't care how juvenile or unprofessional he sounded.

"You two obviously have some things to work out," Alex said. "But Trevor, I don't need to remind you how important this interview is to you and to the

pant leg brushed her bare one.

Her cheeks flushed in response. "I'm good. And yourself? Is life in the city as fun as I imagine?"

"More," he lied. It was cold, lonely, and filled with work—not that he'd give her the satisfaction of that truth. "So. The *News Journal.* I'm impressed."

He'd been rocked when he'd read her interview with Faith Harrington last month, surprised to see her name after all these years. He'd also been proud of her, at least until painful memories replaced the warmth he'd been feeling.

"Thank you. After my divorce, I didn't think I'd get beyond writing obits for the *Serendipity Gazette*, but Faith Harrington changed my life."

Trevor couldn't get past the word *divorce.*

His family, his mother and sister in particular, filled him in on Serendipity gossip, but they'd both learned long ago not to try and feed him information about Lissa. Their phone calls were more enjoyable that way.

"I'm sorry," he said. "About the divorce." Another lie. His heart hadn't stopped pounding in his chest since he'd realized she was free.

"I'm not. It was a long time in coming." She glanced down, then looked at him again. "It wasn't love, Trev. It never was."

Her honest words startled him. From the minute she'd told him she was pregnant with Bradley Banks's baby, all he could think about was that his greatest fear had come true. Lissa had gone out with Brad, the high school quarterback and rich boy, and after they'd broken up, Trevor had made his move on the girl he'd always wanted. Though they'd fallen in love and made plans for the future, he'd still been insecure about his place in her life. Back then he hadn't been able to give her what Brad could, the things she deserved that money could buy.

Not that she'd ever asked for or coveted them, he realized now.

But his inadequacies had always marked him. It was the way of things in Serendipity and his dad, bless him, was the high school janitor. It didn't make Trevor's life easy. So when he and Lissa had a stupid teenage argument, they'd broken up. And when she'd turned back to Brad, even for one night, all Trevor could think was that she'd proven him right. And when she'd ended up pregnant, all hope of fixing things came to an abrupt and ugly end.

Trevor met her gaze. She'd waited quietly as he processed her words. "It's in the past," he said gruffly.

But was it?

"So you'll do the interview?" she asked, hope shining in her eyes.

While he'd been rehashing the pain, she'd been worried about her career. Okay, that made sense. It wasn't like she was here for a personal reason. "Yeah. I'll do it."

"Thank you!" She squealed and impulsively jumped up from her chair, throwing her arms around him in gratitude. In that instant, she was the Lissa he remembered, the full of life, go for the gusto, happy girl he'd fallen for.

And when she pulled him into an embrace, he buried his face in her hair and her familiar scent enveloped him. Desire licked at him, scorching him from the inside out. He remembered how good they'd been together and suddenly he knew what that empty hole was in his life. He missed her, the girl he'd told everything, including his dreams, hopes, and secrets. Since Lissa, he'd never let anyone get that emotionally close, afraid of experiencing that kind of pain and loss again.

She pulled back, an embarrassed flush on her cheeks. "Sorry. I got carried away, but this series of interviews means so much to me. I mean, I didn't think I'd ever get to stop slinging coffee for a living and now…" She trailed off. "I'm rambling."

He laughed for the first time since she'd walked in. "You think?"

He couldn't stop thinking about her words. Serving coffee? Didn't Banks have so much money that after any divorce settlement, she should be able to sit back and eat bonbons if she chose?

Clearly Trevor had a lot to catch up on, and suddenly he wanted to. Now that he'd seen Lissa again, his curiosity was piqued and he wanted the information he'd deliberately ignored over the years. Thinking back to the schedule his secretary had handed him first thing this morning, he figured they had time. Because if Lissa was going to pump him for information about who he was and what made him tick, damned if he wasn't going to do the same thing to her.

"So when do we get started?" he asked her. "On the interview."

Her eyes opened wide. "Right now, if you're ready. I'll do a combination of observing you at work and, when we're alone and you aren't busy, asking questions and talking."

"Now is fine," he said, suddenly revved up and exhilarated. "Did Collette give you a copy of my schedule for the next few days?"

"She handed me a sheet of paper when I walked in. I haven't had time to go over it."

He nodded. "You might want to. There's a formal event on Friday night and a dinner party Saturday," he said, deciding that wherever he was going, so was Lissa.

She paled visibly. "Formal events and dinner parties?"

"All part of the life you need to write about," he reminded her. "What's wrong?"

"It's just that..." She drew a deep breath. "I didn't bring those kinds of dress clothes with me. But I'm staying at the Marriott on Broadway and this is Manhattan, right? I'm sure I'll find something." Her voice trembled and he couldn't understand the cause.

"You sure?"

She nodded, putting on a bright but clearly forced smile. He still knew her well enough to pinpoint that.

"I'll just leave after lunch and go shopping."

"Okay." He narrowed his gaze, knowing that as soon as she left, he'd be on the phone with his mother to find out exactly what had gone on in Lissa's life that he deliberately hadn't wanted to hear.

Now he wanted to know everything.

Trevor didn't understand his sudden turnaround, not completely. But one thing was clear. Their forced time together would provide him with a way to get Lissa out of his system and allow him to move on with his life.

One way or another.

TWO

Lissa checked into her hotel room, needing time to regroup after this morning. No matter how well she thought she'd prepared herself, the meeting had been worse than her most awful nightmare. She'd pictured their reunion often over the years, sometimes in wistful daydreams, more recently since Trevor had become her assignment. In none of them had his explosive reaction been part of the scenario.

Anger she'd accounted for, but one look at his disgusted expression and Lissa's knees had nearly buckled and tears had threatened. Somehow she'd held herself together. Then he'd surprised her again, going from "No fucking way" to all in—and she had to wonder why.

But she couldn't worry about his motives now. She had a full schedule ahead of her. After their initial reunion, Lissa had sat through a typical morning in Trevor's life, which consisted of nonstop phone calls, paperwork, a few confidential meetings for which she'd had to step out of the room, and more phone calls. As a result, she'd had plenty of time to observe him and view the man he'd become.

Of course Lissa had researched her subject and she'd read about Trevor's basic background, much of which she already knew: scholarships to Columbia undergrad and business school, where he'd worked his way through, earning the rest of his way while maintaining stellar grades; internships at the top financial firms in Manhattan; and a job waiting for him when he graduated.

The man was brilliant—something she'd always known—but what he'd accomplished on his own was simply amazing. She was proud of him. So proud, she couldn't stop the warmth fluttering through her even now. But she'd known all about his golden accomplishments and understood his inner drive to make things happen. As a kid, the arrogance he projected had been an act, a cover for insecurities about where he'd come from.

Trevor Dane no longer needed to pretend. An earned confidence had replaced the old cockiness. Sexiness had taken the place of what she'd thought of as hunky hotness.

As for his looks, well, she'd seen recent photos on the company website, but nothing had prepared her for his impact in person. He was gorgeous, the force of his personality magnetic. At a glance, the changes in him were obvious. With his jet-black hair in an expensive cut, a power suit, and a red tie, he radiated confidence. His blue eyes were still as piercing, his knowing gaze as raw. His face was leaner, more chiseled, and if possible, he was even more handsome.

She had no doubt women lined up to date the eligible, wealthy bachelor, something she figured she'd discover first-hand the more time she spent with him. Pain shot through her heart at the thought, but she had no one to blame but herself. No matter how much she was still drawn to him, they were history.

Even after he'd overcome his shock at seeing her, wariness remained between them. Still, he insisted she accompany him, not just for his daily business but on all his after-hours appointments as well.

Beginning with dinner tonight, a formal event on Friday evening, and a dinner party on Saturday. That meant she needed a formal gown and another dress for Saturday night, none of which she could easily afford. She'd tried to cover her surprise and dismay and knew she'd failed miserably... but at least she'd salvaged her pride and hadn't let her lack of money slip.

No doubt Trevor assumed she'd received a nice settlement to end her marriage. She wasn't about to inform him how hard she'd had to scrape for life's little luxuries. Her marriage and its aftermath were none of his business. She didn't want or need his sympathy—if he'd even afford her that, given their history.

She'd left his office at three in order to pull herself together, check into her hotel, and then go shopping. Since she didn't know any places like Consign and Design in the city, she'd have to pay full price at a department store. At least her parents were watching Olivia through the end of this school week and then her baby was going to stay with her father and his bimbo.

Make that Brad's soon-to-be wife, who was all of twenty-two years old and who possessed more money than even Brad's family. Lissa cringed. But no matter how much Lissa resented Brad and his behavior, she knew Olivia was safe and cared for with her father, giving her the freedom to be in the city and take care of business.

She grabbed her purse, made sure she had her credit card in her wallet, and started to leave, when a knock interrupted her. A look through the peephole showed her someone in a hotel uniform, so she opened the door.

"Can I help you?" Lissa asked the younger man.

"Are you Miss Elisabetta Gardelli?" he asked.

She nodded. Every time she heard her full name, she was glad she'd reclaimed her maiden name after the divorce. Olivia was still a Banks, but Elisabetta had no desire to be one anymore.

"Special delivery for you." He gestured to the rolling cart Lissa hadn't noticed before.

She shook her head. "I'm sorry, but I didn't order anything."

The man looked at the paper in his hand. "From Saks Fifth Avenue, for you. May I?" He inclined his head, indicating he wanted to come into the room.

"Umm, sure." Confused, Lissa let him enter and lay out garment bags on the bed, along with shoeboxes and shopping bags.

He'd started to push the cart back out of the room when her brain kicked back into gear. "Wait, please." She went to her wallet and pulled out some bills to tip him with. "Here. Thank you."

"No, ma'am. It's all taken care of, but thank you."

"I don't understand," she said, her legs beginning to shake as she realized there was only one person who knew she needed clothing.

"A Mr. Trevor Dane is downstairs. He asked me to get your permission to share your room number with him?"

Mutely, Lissa nodded. "Send him up," she murmured, lowering herself onto a corner of the bed, knowing her legs wouldn't hold up much longer.

Nothing about this interview and reunion with

Trevor was going as she'd envisioned. She'd known being with him again would be challenging, but she'd hoped it would be cathartic. She'd never quite gotten him out of her system and after seeing him today, she was coming to the conclusion she never would. She thought she'd be resigning herself to that throughout this long, torturous weekend.

But now she was facing this… thoughtful, caring gesture from a man who ought to hate her. He should be doing everything he could to make her time with him as painless for himself as possible—by spending as little time with her as he needed to in order to get the article written. Yet he was sending her expensive clothing from Saks and showing up at her hotel room in the middle of his workday to… what?

She had no idea, and that scared her.

* * *

As Trevor rode the elevator to the thirty-sixth floor, he figured he'd lost his mind. He had no other explanation for doing something so out of character as leaving work in the middle of the day. No doubt about it, though, his phone call with his mother had shaken him badly.

For years he'd assumed that once Lissa had gotten pregnant and Brad had done the right thing by marrying her, she'd lived a charmed life as Bradley

Banks's wife. The money, the country club, all the things that at the time, Trevor could never be sure he'd be able to provide. And once she'd had Brad's baby and married him, whether or not Trevor succeeded in life no longer mattered. He'd had a decade to build a picture in his mind of how good her life had been without him, while no matter how much professional success he achieved, Trevor still felt hollow inside.

It had taken no time to have his illusions—or rather, delusions—shattered. According to his mother, Lissa's married life had been a decade-long embarrassment. The bastard had married her in name only, doing the so-called "right thing" by his child. Not by the baby's mother. When Lissa finally had enough and walked out, her settlement had been paltry and she'd been forced to take a part-time job serving coffee at Cuppa Café while writing the obituary column for the *Serendipity Gazette*. She lived in a small house on her original side of town, and though their daughter's future was secure thanks to Brad's parents, Lissa worked for everything she had.

No wonder she'd nearly passed out when he'd mentioned a formal affair and a dinner party this weekend. Not only couldn't she afford those kinds of clothes, she probably didn't even own them. Trevor had misjudged her, the life she'd lived, and who she'd become. And though nothing could change what had happened in the past, he damned well respected her choices now.

He should have known better. If he could have gotten past his hurt and anger sooner and let his mother fill him in, he'd have known how unhappy her life had to be. Would it have changed anything? Would he have gone back for her, married or not?

He'd never know.

On that thought, a mechanical voice announced he was on the thirty-sixth floor, and the elevator door opened in front of him.

Well, whatever was in the past, Lissa was here now and Trevor had this one chance to see what might have been. What could be. Either way, when this interview process was over, he'd have the one thing that had been missing all these years.

Closure.

And he'd also have Lissa one more time. He refused to accept any other outcome.

Trevor reached Lissa's room and found the door partially open. He walked in to find her sitting on the edge of the bed surrounded by bags of clothing.

"Hi," he said to capture her attention.

She glanced up, meeting his gaze with a wide-eyed, wary gaze. "What is all this? And don't say *clothes*," she said, before he could do just that. "Why didn't you just let me go shopping?"

Trevor ran a hand through his hair, embarrassed. It wasn't like he went around ordering clothing for women. "It wasn't hard to figure out that I was putting you on the spot with the formal affair and the dinner party."

"And I said I'd go shopping."

"You also mentioned something about serving coffee and you literally paled when it dawned on you that you'd have to buy new things. I realized I knew nothing about you now." He stared up at the ceiling, knowing he had no choice but to admit the truth. "So I called my mother and she filled me in."

Lissa felt her face flush hot with embarrassment and awkwardness. "So you found out all about my life and realized I couldn't really afford a new wardrobe for the weekend. You felt sorry for me and sent these clothes over?" Her voice rose along with her mortification.

"Hey, that's not it." He sat down beside her, close enough so their legs were touching. "It's more like I got a shocking lesson in making assumptions."

She swallowed hard. "You thought I lived well off the Banks money."

"Well, I assumed that if the guy was doing the right thing by marrying you after he—" He caught himself before saying *knocked you up*. "After he got you pregnant, then he would treat you right after he split up with you, too."

"You know what they say about someone who assumes things," she muttered.

To her surprise, he laughed. "Yep. And an ass certainly describes how I acted today. So maybe the clothes were an apology, too."

Lissa didn't know what to do with this kinder, gentler Trevor, and part of her wondered if that wasn't his intention. To keep her off balance, guessing, unsure of herself during the time she was with him. To her dismay, she realized she didn't know him all that well anymore.

"I'm sorry things have been so hard for you."

She forced a smile. "I managed." She'd also put herself in the position of having to marry Brad, but it didn't seem smart to get into the specifics of their past right now. "Thank you, though."

"You're welcome."

"And thank you for these." She swept her hand toward the bags surrounding them on the bed.

"That was my pleasure." His smile warmed her straight down to her toes.

She was trying really hard not to think about the fact that they were sitting in a hotel room alone on a king-sized bed, but it wasn't easy. Trevor's pants-clad thigh touched her bare one and she could swear she felt the heat of his skin through the material. When she inhaled, he smelled deliciously male and need rose quickly.

It had been so long since she'd had a man's arms around her, a man who made her feel good and wanted. Unlike her ex, Lissa had remained faithful in her marriage, and her one short relationship afterward had left her cold and wondering whether she'd ever feel real desire again.

Well, now she knew. She ought to be surprised that it was Trevor who'd awakened her long-dormant hormones, but she wasn't. Not really.

Lissa pulled in a deep breath and forced herself to continue the conversation. For all she knew, she was the only one feeling the heat and she didn't want him to think she'd misinterpret a kind gesture for anything more. She knew how he felt about her.

His first unguarded reaction had shown his true emotions, and though he was trying to be nice now, she knew the resentment still lurked below the surface. She couldn't let herself think anything else was at play or she'd be risking her heart. She was sure Trevor's was locked up tight, at least to her.

"How did you know my size?" she asked.

He shrugged. "I asked my secretary to guess. Some of the things will have to be returned."

She nodded. "I look forward to trying them on."

"I look forward to seeing you in them." His gorgeous eyes sparkled at the thought.

"What time should I be ready tonight?"

"I'll pick you up at seven."

Lissa shook her head. "I'll meet you there." This wasn't a date; it was business. She couldn't let him play the gentleman and go through the motions. It would only make her want things she'd never have.

He scowled. "I don't mind picking you up."

"There's no need for you to treat me like a date. I'm a journalist writing your story," she felt compelled to remind him. Or maybe she needed to say it out loud for herself. "The Waldorf, correct?"

He nodded, but she could see from the stiffness in his shoulders he wasn't happy with her suggestion.

"Great," she said, rising from the bed. "I'll see you there."

He rose and stood way too close. "You'll see me, all right," he murmured too enigmatically for her liking. Reaching out, he placed his fingers beneath her chin until she looked directly into his eyes. "We have a lot to catch up on."

He tipped his head and her stomach did a nervous roll as his lips came closer to hers. A yearning the likes of which she'd never felt before rose up to greet him. But instead of touching his mouth to hers, he placed a kiss on her cheek, his touch too short to make any promises and yet too long to mean nothing.

He stared at her for a long while afterward, as if studying her.

She curled her hands into fists at her sides, her heart pounding, her body responding in ways she'd long forgotten. Her breasts grew full, her nipples peaked, and dampness pooled between her thighs.

"See you later," he said in a deep voice, gruffer than before.

"Bye," she whispered, unable to form a coherent thought. And though he hadn't really kissed her or touched her at all, heat licked at her from the inside out.

Oh boy, was she in trouble.

Lissa spent the rest of the afternoon pulling herself together. She tried on the variety of dresses Collette had sent over, surprised to find each one fit. It was up to her to decide which to wear and which to return. The answer came down to one question.

How sexy did she want to be?

She luxuriated in a scented bath and took an amazing amount of time getting herself ready. The last time she'd primped so much on her appearance had been back in high school. Sadly, that had been the last time she'd truly cared about impressing someone, and she had to admit it felt too good to make the attempt now.

Though she knew she ought to eat and had ordered up something light, she merely picked at the salad and fruit, too nervous for a full meal. Still, at least she had something in her stomach so that she could nurse a drink and not feel tipsy. Something told her she'd need to be in full control of her faculties this evening when dealing with Trevor. Not to mention, she wouldn't be taking notes on the people she met and on Trevor's interactions, so she'd need to rely on memory when she wrote up her interview notes later.

Finally, gown and shoes chosen, she gathered her evening bag—another smart choice by Collette—and headed downstairs to hail a cab. Except when she reached the lobby, she found Trevor waiting for her.

Standing against a pillar, clad in a perfectly fitted tuxedo, the man exuded confidence and sex appeal. She was so surprised to see him, so affected by his masculinity, that she nearly tripped in her high heels as she made her way over to him.

"I thought I said I'd meet you there," she said.

"And I told you you'd see me. I just didn't say where." His gaze raked over her, hot and heated, devouring her with its intensity. "You look gorgeous."

"Thank you. Collette chose well." She managed to speak though her mouth was bone dry.

"It's not the clothes, Lissa. It's you," he said gruffly. "Do you know how many times I wished I could afford to buy you nice things?"

He was talking about ten years ago.

She smiled. "I never wanted them," she murmured. She'd only wanted him. She shook her head, shaking off the memories they couldn't change.

"Ready to go?" he asked, placing a strong hand against her bare back. "The limo is waiting."

Surprised, she opened her mouth, then closed it again. "Limo?" The word sounded like a squeak and he grinned.

"Your article is supposed to document who I am and how I live, correct?" She nodded. "Don't worry. It's not a full limo. It's a town car with a driver." He chuckled, probably at her shocked expression.

"Lead the way," she said, raising her chin in a futile attempt at nonchalance.

The man was riding roughshod over every one of her good intentions and damned if she wasn't enjoying having someone else take control for a change.

Not that she'd give him the satisfaction of telling him that. All she had to do now was get through the rest of the night without succumbing to that charm he seemed so determined to lavish on her.

But that was the sensible Elisabetta talking. The old Elisabetta—the one who would follow Trevor's lead to hell and back, the one who was enjoying the feel of his heated palm against her back—urged her to stop thinking and enjoy. Not that she'd forget why she was with Trevor or that she had an article to write when her time with him was through, but for now, the devil on her shoulder insisted she relax and see where this night and these sparks between them would lead.

And she wondered which Lissa would win.

THREE

For Trevor, nothing about tonight was work-related. The fundraiser was something his firm believed in and attendance was mandatory, but nobody conducted business at these kinds of events. Most attended with their husbands, wives, or significant others and it was as much a chance for people to catch up personally as it was to raise money for the charity. Normally Trevor hated these things. He'd have to dig up a date, either a woman who bored him to tears or one who thought she could be the one to catch him when no other woman had been able to before.

At first he'd questioned why this was on the reporter's schedule of events, but he realized Alex wanted to showcase both Trevor and the firm's commitment to altruistic causes. He'd resigned himself to sucking it up because at least he'd be with a woman who had no expectations. Once he'd discovered the reporter was Lissa and after he'd made the deliberate decision to let go of the past for this short time they were together, he'd begun to look forward to the evening.

As for her insistence that she'd take a cab? It was easier to let her think she'd gotten her way than to argue. And it had been worth the waiting time in the lobby to get his first glimpse of her uncensored expression the moment she'd laid eyes on him as she walked out of the elevator. Pure, unadulterated pleasure lit her gaze, along with a definite dose of female appreciation, before wariness shuttered her emotions. And her skin glowed radiantly, her emerald eyes twinkling with delight she tried hard to hide.

It was enough for him to know he'd gotten to her the same way she affected him.

Only then did he allow himself the full pleasure of viewing her in all her glory. Dressed in a gold gown, Grecian in design, that draped over one shoulder and hugged her curves in all the right places, she looked like a princess. The back dipped enticingly low, giving him a glimpse of her olive skin and affording the perfect place to settle his palm possessively against her back.

They made the ride to the Waldorf in silence and Trevor let her squirm. He knew she was questioning his motives and what he wanted from her. He liked her nervous and a bit wary. That was when she'd be most unguarded, letting little things slip.

There was much to revisit, much still unsaid, and

though they had a limited amount of time together, most of it would be one on one. Just not right away.

As soon as they arrived at the hotel and walked into the ballroom, all eyes turned to look at them. Trevor understood. Lissa, with her Mediterranean olive skin, jet black hair, and green eyes, made an impression. She had a regal look and he was proud to have her on his arm.

"I'm the envy of every man here," he said, escorting her toward the bar.

"Flatterer. Have you seen the other women here? They're at least twenty pounds lighter and have much tinier waists," she said, laughing without seeming uncomfortable.

"I hadn't noticed. I can't take my eyes off you." He drew a deep breath. "Would you like a drink?"

She nodded. "A glass of white wine."

The bartender had heard her, so Trevor merely added, "And a Scotch on the rocks for me."

A few minutes later, they had their drinks in hand. "Let's walk," he said, steering her into the crowds. The sooner they did the obligatory meet and greet, the sooner Trevor could dance with this woman and take her to bed. They passed the next thirty minutes talking to the important people at Wittman Financial and other people in the industry. Trevor was careful to introduce Lissa to the movers and shakers by both name and company affiliation, knowing that despite the personal nature of their time together, when all was said and done, she had a job to do.

"Trevor, Ms. Gardelli, I'm so glad you could make it." Trevor turned at the sound of Alexander's voice. "I see you two have worked out your… differences?"

"It's a pleasure to see you again, Mr. Wittman," Lissa said, extending her free hand.

Instead of shaking it, Alex lifted her hand and placed a courtly kiss on top. "You look ravishing."

Lissa blushed.

"I was just telling her the same thing myself," Trevor said, unable to hide his pleasure at being with her.

Over the years, as Trevor had escorted various dates to these types of evenings, he'd envied Bradley Banks, thinking the man was taking Lissa to country club events, showing her off and then taking her home and making love to her.

Trevor's stomach turned at the thought even now.

How much time had he wasted by not finding out the truth of how her life had been?

Which reminded him, he had some crow to eat. He turned to Alex. "I already apologized to Lissa and now it's your turn. I was shocked to see her after all these years and I let emotion cloud my judgment. I was rude earlier today and I apologize."

Trevor wasn't a man prone to saying *I'm sorry*, but

in this case, he owed his boss and mentor and intended to prove he understood his mistake.

"I don't know what happened between you two in the past, but to have such an explosive reaction means great passion was involved."

A small hiccup came from Lissa, a clear sign of shock.

"Alex…" Trevor said in warning.

The other man waved away Trevor's concerns because in Alex's world, people were meant to be paired off. He was a romantic to the bone.

"Speaking of passion, Emma sends her best, but she's home with a headache and she wants to make sure she's better for tomorrow night's dinner party. Which means I'll be leaving early," he said with regret.

"I hope she feels better," Lissa said. "I'm looking forward to meeting her tomorrow."

Trevor stepped closer to Lissa and slid an arm around her waist. She stiffened for a moment before managing to relax. "Please send Emma my best wishes. And we'll see her tomorrow," Trevor added.

"She's looking forward to it, as am I." Alex nodded. His perceptive gaze locked on Trevor's possessive hold on Lissa and a smug grin settled on the man's face. "I'll see you two later," Alex said and headed off to finish making his rounds.

Trevor gave Lissa a few minutes to enjoy her drink

in silence and take in the ambiance in the ballroom. He finished his and turned to face her.

"Dance?" he asked.

"Sure." Lissa handed her wine glass to a passing server.

Lissa steeled herself for the next few minutes in Trevor's arms.

It was hard enough to see the heat and appreciation in his eyes whenever he looked at her. Harder still to make herself believe he meant it. She didn't doubt he wanted her. She desired him just as much. It was how she felt about that look in his eyes that frightened her. As he wrapped his arm around her waist and pulled her close, the warmth of his body and the thrill his touch inspired scared her even more.

Yet when he looked down and into her eyes, she practically melted on the spot.

"This feels familiar," he said as he slowly moved to the strains of the music.

She laughed, remembering their junior prom. They hadn't made it to their senior. "As I recall, we were more awkward then."

He shrugged. "Practice makes perfect." He stroked her bare back with his thumb and she shivered.

"Do you come to these things often?" she asked.

"It's part of the job. There are charitable galas, holiday parties, things like that."

"And that's where you got all your practice. Who were your partners?" she asked, forcing a smile while they talked.

"Is that on the record? Or more of a personal question?"

She tried to pull away but he tightened his hold, continuing their glide around the dance floor. "Well?"

"I think you know."

He nodded. "I do. And the answer is, nameless, unimportant women."

Her heart stopped beating. "All of them?"

Again, he nodded.

"Why?" she asked softly, unable to believe they were having this conversation.

"Are you sure you want an answer?"

Was she sure? Ten years of wondering if Trevor ever thought of her. Lonely nights of imagining him taking other women to bed, falling in love with one of them, eventually marrying one and having children. Jealousy had eaten away at her even as her rational self knew she had no right. She was the one who'd turned to someone else. She'd had another man's baby.

She met his gaze and nodded.

"Okay, but once you get it, there's no turning back."

She couldn't suppress a smile. Because she had the sense there was no turning back anyway. "I'm sure."

His dark eyes smoldered with need. "They were all nameless, unimportant blurs because they weren't you."

"Oh, Trevor," she said as his words wrapped around her heart.

His grip on her waist tightened, his large hand cupping her so hard she thought he'd leave marks. The thought of him marking her in any way aroused her beyond reason. So did the hardened erection pressing into her belly, telling her how very much he wanted her.

That was what she could believe in. The only thing.

The feelings behind the desire? Those were emotions she no longer let herself trust.

"I need to get out of here," he said gruffly.

Lissa nodded. She'd never wanted anything more. Another night with Trevor was more than she'd ever imagined—and now it looked like they'd have at least two before she went home to Serendipity and the life she'd chosen so very long ago.

*　　*　　*

Instead of going to Lissa's hotel as she'd expected, Trevor gave the driver his Upper East Side address, which for some reason made this next step seem all too real. To see where he lived, what his life was like...

She shivered.

"Cold?" he asked from his seat beside her in the car. She shook her head. "Ah. Then you're thinking too much."

She smiled, amazed he could read her so well after all these years.

"Guess I'll have to remedy that." He reached up and slid his fingers beneath her hair, cupping her neck and pulling her close. Then, without wasting any time, he sealed his lips over hers.

His instincts had been correct, she thought. At the sizzling connection between them, all coherent thought stopped completely.

He'd always been talented with his mouth and that hadn't changed. His lips slid back and forth over hers, taking her for a blissful, mind-numbing experience that quickly turned hot and arousing when he grasped her hair in his hand and deepened the kiss.

The slightly aggressive move was somehow erotic too, and her body liquefied with the tug against her scalp. With a moan, she returned each swipe and thrust of his tongue with equal fervor and need, wanting nothing more than to crawl into his lap and get as close as possible given the barrier of clothing.

When he suddenly pulled back, her entire body protested the loss of his mouth over hers. "What's wrong?" she asked, feeling dazed and unfulfilled.

"We're here," he said.

Lissa looked out the window. "Oh," she said, shocked to see the car had stopped in front of a building.

He grinned and slipped his hand in hers. "Thank you, Tony," he said to the driver.

Lissa blushed and ducked her head, embarrassed they'd been making out with the man right in front.

"He's paid to be discreet," Trevor said, laughing, making Lissa wonder if he made this a habit, seducing his dates on their way home.

She didn't want to know if he did.

More sober now, she followed him inside, aware of his arm around her waist but not feeling as relaxed as she had earlier. Which was ridiculous, all things considered.

He lived in a building with a doorman, which meant another stranger to nod to as she passed by, walking with Trevor to the elevator. They stepped off on the twenty-first floor and headed down the long, lit corridor to the end of the hall.

He unlocked the door and motioned for her to step in ahead of him. He'd left lights on and she was able to look around immediately. He tossed his keys on a shelf in the entryway before taking her hand and pulling her into the main living room. A wall of windows overlooked the glittering skyline of Manhattan.

"The view is incredible," she said as she walked to the windows.

In fact, the entire apartment was a thing of masculine beauty, with its heavy, rugged furniture facing an oversized wall-mounted television, shelves with books and other decorator chosen pieces, and picture frames. It was the photographs that gave the place a lived-in, homey touch and at a glance, Lissa recognized the various photos of Trevor's family, his parents, his sister and her husband, and their new baby.

"The view is the reason I chose this place. There's no highrise to either block my visibility or give anyone an unobstructed look into my private space. I can leave the shades open most of the time." He stepped up beside her and she immediately felt his body heat.

"Do you miss living in Serendipity? The wide open spaces?" she asked, wondering if she could give up small-town living for Manhattan.

"I miss some things more than others," he said in a deep voice.

Taking her off guard, he moved around her and wrapped his arms around her waist. His front pressed into her back and he cuddled her in his embrace, a feeling that made her feel so safe and secure that warning bells went off in her head.

But she couldn't bring herself to heed them. His

warm breath fanned across her neck while his impressive erection pulsed against her backside, as together they looked over the brightly lit city.

God, she'd dreamed about this.

About the day he'd come back for her and make everything right in her world. Except then she'd been a naïve young woman, despite her pregnancy, still too much of a teenager to understand what she'd done to her life. She was a woman now and knew better than to put stock in adolescent dreams, but for this one night and maybe tomorrow, he could be hers again. Nobody would begrudge her some new and better memories to keep with her on lonely nights.

Not wanting to waste a second more, she turned, looping her arms around his neck and looking into his eyes. "Kiss me," she said, deciding to take what she desired—and what he obviously wanted as well.

Trevor had been worried she'd come to her senses and change her mind, so he didn't need a second invitation now. Cupping her face in his hands, he backed her against the plate glass windows and kissed her long and hard, so deeply she couldn't mistake his desire. He swept his tongue inside her mouth and everything in his world righted itself once more. He teased her, brushing his tongue back and forth, relearning her touch, her taste, her scent, the way she felt.

Back when they were kids, they'd spent hours kissing as though nothing else mattered and they had all the time they'd ever want together. Though he knew better now, he could still kiss her for hours. Only her.

With other women, he'd rush through the foreplay and get to the deed because, ironically, he'd always found the preliminaries more intimate, more telling about someone's feelings. Post-Lissa, knowing he'd closed his emotions off, he'd made it his mission to arouse his partner quickly and leave her satisfied, but with no question that he wasn't lingering before or after. The women he was with knew the score. It was a reputation he'd perfected, and though he wasn't proud of it, at least he was honest.

He was equally so now. He began to thrust his tongue deeper into her mouth, mimicking the act his hardened body craved with near desperation. Lissa moaned and hooked one leg around his, arching her pelvis into him and pulling him tighter against her. The small circles she made with her hips drove him insane and the barrier of clothing nearly killed him.

Still kissing her, with one hand he reached for the side zipper of her gown and eased it down as far as he could manage. With the other, he yanked the silky material off her shoulder.

She wiggled her upper body and the entire gown

pooled around her on the floor. Needing the visual, he finally broke the kiss and stepped back to admire her, but no sooner had they separated than she reached up to cross her arms and cover herself.

"Uh-uh." He grabbed her wrists and pulled them away from her body. "Keep them down there," he said in a voice he barely recognized.

She'd always had gorgeous, voluptuous breasts and that hadn't changed. He brushed his thumb over her already distended nipple and she let out a sound, half sigh, half groan as it hardened even more beneath his fingertip. Then he did the same to the other breast. A brief touch and it, too, puckered for him.

Trevor grinned. "Still so damned sensitive."

"And yet you're taking your time and torturing me," she said in a shaky voice.

"I'm savoring you." Her entire body trembled but he wasn't finished. Before she could react again, he cupped her full breast in his hand and lifted it to his waiting mouth.

Her skin smelled like peaches and she tasted sweeter than he remembered. He savored one nipple thoroughly, nipping, teasing, blowing cool air over the puckered tip before moving to the other one and giving it the same care. By the time he was finished, her head was thrown back against the window, her hips bucking forward seeking relief.

His dick felt as if it would shatter at any moment and for him, this part of the foreplay was over. "Bed, sweetheart?" He held out his hand.

She looked at him with glazed eyes and nodded, placing her hand inside his. He helped her step out of the dress surrounding her and realized she still wore high-heeled crystal-looking sandals, a matching pair of panties... and nothing more.

Her stomach, while not flat, fit with the rest of her curves and he wondered how he'd gone so long without feeling her surrounding him, becoming a part of him.

He led her to the bedroom, aware she was naked and uncomfortable but doing her best not to show it. As soon as they reached the bed, he stripped off his clothes, not wanting to wait another second to feel the heat of her skin flush against his. But when she reached to remove her sandals, he shook his head.

She narrowed her gaze. "Seriously?"

He grinned. "What can I say? It's been a fantasy of mine, fucking you while you're wearing nothing but endlessly high heels."

"You fantasized about me?" she asked, sounding well and truly shocked.

His heart nearly stopped but the admission was out there. "Nobody else has ever done it for me the way you do."

She opened her mouth and he used the opportunity to settle his naked body over hers and stop any further conversation. They'd have to talk, but it wasn't happening now.

He let his weight ease against her, gritting his teeth as he came into contact with her damp heat. "Oh, baby." He cupped her hips in his hand and ground himself against her.

"You don't play fair," she murmured, her arms coming around him.

"Why? Because I don't want to talk anymore?" He braced his hands on either side of her and buried his face between her neck and shoulder, first merely kissing her, then using his teeth, tugging hard until she moaned and bucked beneath him.

"I don't want to talk, either." She bent her legs, making room for him. "I need you inside me."

He lifted his head and looked into her eyes, dying for exactly the same thing. "Do I need protection?"

She shook her head, her pretty green eyes wide and glassy. "I'm on the pill."

His body trembled at the thought of entering her bareback.

"You?" she asked.

"I'm safe. I've never had sex without one," he assured her. He'd only asked now because it was Lissa, and more than anything he wanted to feel all of her when he was finally inside her again.

She drew a deep breath. "Well you don't have to worry about me, either. It's been so long I'll be lucky if I remember how," she said, forcing a laugh he knew she didn't feel.

He brushed her tangled hair off her cheek. "Nobody since your divorce?" he asked her, surprised yet oddly pleased.

She bit her lip before finally speaking. "Nobody since not long after my marriage."

Trevor ignored the thrill the admission brought, knowing it was selfish to be happy she'd been so alone, yet pleased she hadn't been with anyone but him and the ex he refused to think about.

Lissa sighed. "After the divorce I dated one guy—you might remember Russ Mason—but I couldn't bring myself to be with him that way."

Trevor hated talking about any other men, but he knew it was necessary. He cocked an eyebrow in question.

"Just no desire." She blushed, but he appreciated her honesty and kissed her cheek. "Anyway, the relationship ended quickly after that. Russ thought I was frigid and frankly, I didn't care." She lifted her shoulder in a delicate shrug.

Unable to hold it in, Trevor barked out a laugh.

"What's so funny?" She frowned at him.

"Any guy who thinks you're frigid must need lessons. You're so hot you're burning me alive," he told her, meaning every word. "Watch."

Dipping his head, he licked at first one nipple, then the next. Those rosy peaks were quickly becoming his favorite part of her because she was so damned responsive. One touch and she grew immediately slick and wet, which he intended to show her. As he reached down and slid his finger through her moist folds, her hips arched up and into him, seeking deeper penetration.

"Soon," he promised her. First he came up with the proof to back up his claim. "See? So not frigid."

Her genuine smile nearly undid him. Her words finished the task. "It's you, Trev. It's always been you."

Unable to hold back any longer, he raised himself over her. "I can't promise slow and easy," he said, apologizing ahead of time.

"Then it's a good thing hard and fast suits me just fine." She clasped his erection in her hand, rubbing her fingertip over the moisture pooled at the tip.

He gritted his teeth, nearly coming from the intense pleasure of her touch as she guided him toward her slick heat. Only when he was poised at her entry did she release her hold so he could ease his aching shaft inside her.

She was tight and hot and he tried desperately to at least start slowly.

"You promised you wouldn't take it slow." She rocked her lower body and snapped the last of his self-control.

It hadn't been difficult to do. Even though he'd tried not to let himself remember them or consciously think of her, he hadn't lied when he'd said she was and remained his greatest fantasy.

FOUR

Lissa didn't do sex without emotion. Even the one time, when she'd conceived her daughter, she'd been an emotional mess because she was seventeen, turning eighteen in a few months, tipsy, hurt, and filled with the knowledge that Brad wasn't Trevor. Though she often came off hard and edgy to the outside world, inside she was one big mush afraid of being hurt.

Despite the easy banter with Trevor, despite her self-made promise to hold on to her heart, the minute he entered her, filling her body in the way only he ever had, he broke down her walls and she knew she'd have one hell of a time putting them back up.

"Okay, sweetheart?" He paused to let her body accommodate him, the strain of holding back showing in his face.

So did the play of emotions in his expression telling her he felt it too—the fusing of their bodies with no barrier between them. He was marking her and she feared she'd never be the same.

"I'm good," she said, concentrating on feeling, not

thinking. And he felt incredible, hot and thick inside her. "You won't hurt me." To encourage him, she lifted her head and pulled his earlobe into her mouth, teasing and tugging with her teeth.

With a groan, he released the hold he'd been keeping and began a steady thrust inside her. Her mind fogged. Her body pulsed, a wave of pleasure rose inside her and she reached out to grab it, to meet and match his rhythm, but the shoes and their spiked heels held her back, preventing her from digging her feet into the mattress for purchase.

She moaned in frustration, her body in desperate need of more than the delicious glide of his hard erection deep into her. She needed to feel him slam into her, to make her his.

As if he knew and understood, he changed his position slightly and adjusted his motion, twisting his hips each time his body connected with hers. That did it. Every thrust brought his pubic bone down hard against just the right spot and he took her higher with each successive plunge deeper inside her. Braced on his arms, he stared into her eyes, watching her as he possessed her—body, mind, and soul.

Frantic to hold onto some semblance of self, to hold something back from him, she closed her eyes and—the delicious movement ceased.

He stopped moving completely.

Lissa cried out, digging her nails into his shoulders, urging him on.

"Not until you look at me," he said, his tone harsh.

She forced her eyelids open and met his dark, sexy gaze. "I hate you," she muttered.

"No, you just wish you did." And then he began to make love to her once more.

He played her body as though he knew it intimately, taking her higher as he grew impossibly bigger and harder, powering into her with deep, heavy thrusts. She was wet, she was needy, and he satisfied every craving she had, the waves of desire rising higher in her body.

Yeah, she'd had self-induced orgasms over the years, but they paled in comparison to having this man in control. He slowed when she neared completion, letting her body wind down only to hammer home harder again, building her need and promising a spectacular climax he kept just out of reach.

She whimpered, raising her hips, clenching him tighter inside her, holding onto him until the slick moisture of their connection sounded in the room, an erotic accompaniment to the music they were already making together.

Warmth, heat, and a sweet bombardment of sensations swept through her at lightning speed, growing in intensity, the ultimate prize almost within reach.

"Come, sweetheart, because I sure as hell am." With that, he thrust deep and up high, twisting his hips and taking her exactly where she wanted to be.

Lissa came right then, her body so in tune with him she exploded on command. She screamed, bucking against him as the most amazing sensations rocked her world. Suddenly, he tensed above her and shouted her name, his muscles clenching, his hips continuing a pump and grind that sent her body into another round of mini detonations that seemed never to end.

He collapsed on top of her, breathing hard, and she savored his weight and the warmth of his damp skin. "I may never recover," she said, only half joking.

"Me neither." With a grunt, he rolled over and she felt the loss of contact too keenly. He leaned over and pressed a quick kiss on her lips before rising and heading into the bathroom.

She rid herself of her sandals just as he returned, not giving her a chance to decide whether to dress and get out quickly or succumb to the urge to wrap herself in his arms and fall asleep.

Still naked, he climbed in beside her and pulled her into his embrace. That answered that question, she thought, and snuggled in. Neither spoke, and to her amazement, she didn't feel the need or the absence of conversation. His actions spoke volumes and she wanted to enjoy the time she had left.

Not wanting to dwell on the inevitability of their parting, she forced herself to operate as she always did when falling asleep. She turned her mind to work and deadlines. As far as Trevor was concerned, her story was nearly complete. She had already researched his background beyond what she knew personally. And between watching him in the office, spending an evening with him at a fundraiser, and then being given a first-hand view of his apartment, she possessed a broad glimpse into other facets of Trevor as a man. A few more specific questions would fill out the missing pieces.

As she went through things in her mind, she was acutely aware of his breathing and knew the minute he fell asleep, his hold on her loosening only slightly, his breaths coming deeper and more evenly. She relaxed into his rhythm, letting exhaustion claim her.

Her body was sated, her eyelids were already growing heavy, and her last thought before drifting off was of how easily she could get used to falling asleep in his arms.

* * *

Trevor couldn't bring himself to move. An early riser with no need for an alarm clock, he had never put in blackout shades, preferring to wake up on his own or, on the occasions he slept in, to the warm sun on his face.

This morning, his internal clock woke him and he immediately became aware of two things: Lissa was in his bed, her warm, naked body draped over his; and it was Saturday and there wasn't any place he had to be. Nothing to interrupt something he'd dreamed about since he was sixteen.

Waking up with this woman in his arms.

He was hard and he couldn't attribute it to a typical morning. Not when one female thigh was slung over his and the scent he now associated with her filled every breath.

He nuzzled beneath her jaw and licked the skin along her neck. She moaned softly, coming awake slowly, so he continued to nibble at her skin, taking his time as she became aware.

"Trev?" she asked in a sleepy voice.

He raised an eyebrow. "Expecting someone else?" he asked, laughing.

She didn't lift her head or meet his gaze. "You feel good," she murmured.

"So do you." He closed his eyes, wondering how to make this last longer than the course of the interview.

He didn't bring women home often and when he did, they didn't sleep over. It didn't matter whether or not he had to drive them home, he never wanted to wake up with someone he'd have to politely get rid of the next day.

When it came to Lissa, he never wanted to let her go.

Before he could continue with that train of thought, a noise sounded from the other room, muted but still clear enough to be heard. "Mom. Mom. Mom. Mom. Mummy. Mummy. Mum. Mum…"

"What the hell is that?" he asked as Lissa popped out of his arms.

"My cell," she said. "It's my daughter's text message alert. It's Stewie from *Family Guy*."

Nude, she rose from the bed, distracting him from the obvious—the reminder of her daughter. But suddenly she glanced at the uncovered windows and then at him, her cheeks red.

Personally, he could look at her all day. "I have a T-shirt in the top drawer." He gestured to a wooden chest and she shot him a grateful look.

A few seconds later, her gorgeous body was covered in an oversized white shirt that was sheer enough to allow him a thrill but made her more comfortable as she headed into the other room, returning with her small purse.

And that quickly, reality resurfaced. He was no longer in the solitary bubble he'd created for the two of them, and for the first time since laying eyes on her yesterday, the old wounds and sharp pain sliced him in the chest once more. But he was also able to remind himself that the pain was a decade old, and that was a first.

She pulled out her phone. "Olivia—I call her Livvy—is at her father's for the weekend," Lissa said as she hit some buttons, obviously looking at the text message. "Or not." She let out a groan.

"What's wrong?" Trevor asked.

"Her text says *Have a cold*. And *At grandma's*. I need to call my mother."

"How do you know she didn't mean the Bankses?" Trevor must be growing up, because here he was, suddenly curious about her relationships and family dynamics.

"Because Livvy calls Lyla *Grandmother* Banks." Lissa wrinkled her nose at the formal term.

Trevor agreed. "What a bunch of assholes," he muttered, rising to his feet.

Before Lissa could react or reply, she gestured to the phone. "Hi, Mom. It's me. Livvy's with you?"

While Lissa was busy, Trevor escaped into the bathroom to wash up and regroup while he was at it. He splashed cold water on his face and brushed his teeth, stalling while he pulled himself together. Talk about being in complete denial for the last twenty-four hours. While he'd been losing himself in Lissa, thinking he'd found the missing pieces of his heart, he'd somehow managed to completely block out the thing that had broken them up to begin with.

Her daughter.

Brad's daughter. He shoved that thought away before he could dwell on it too long.

The fact that she lived in Serendipity, and he lived here.

Hell, if he kept thinking, he was sure he'd come up with a whole lot more things that could keep them apart.

Trevor stepped out of the bathroom in time to hear, "Hey, baby."

Lissa spoke into the phone, her tone warm, sweet, and filled with pure love. A tone Trevor had never heard from her before and despite himself, he was intrigued.

He grabbed a clean pair of underwear and jeans, dressing while she finished her call. "No, baby, I'm not coming home until tomorrow. You have a cold and grandma's going to take good care of you, okay?" She grew silent, then said, "I love you, too. Bye."

Clearly bracing herself, she straightened her shoulders and met his gaze. "Sorry about that."

Trevor shook his head. "No need to apologize for reality," he said. "Kids need their mothers." And their fathers, which brought up another question nagging at him. "If she has a cold, why didn't Brad just keep her with him?"

She frowned. "My guess? Sunny doesn't want to catch it. That's Brad's fiancée. She's twenty-two and more of a child than Livvy," Lissa said with a roll of her eyes.

"Does Livvy look like you? Or her father?"

Lissa blinked, obviously startled at his question. So was he. But he wanted to know, even as he knew the answer might hurt.

"My mom thinks she looks exactly like me."

The vise squeezing his chest eased. "Then she must be beautiful."

"She is." Despite the obvious awkwardness of the subject, her eyes glowed with pride and happiness over her daughter.

Her pleasure was contagious, sparking a flame to life inside him. One he wanted to squelch and fan at the same time. But he'd come this far. He'd made love to her. If he turned back now, he'd never know what could be.

"Do you have a picture?"

She nodded. Reaching for her purse once more, she pulled out her phone and showed him the background photo. A beautiful girl with Lissa's green eyes, black hair, and olive complexion stared back at him with her mother's wide smile, squeezing something inside his chest.

"She's gorgeous," he said, his voice thick.

"Thanks. I think so, but I'm biased." She closed her phone and slid it back into her bag.

"Lissa?"

"Hmm?" She looked up, a curious expression on her face.

"Do you remember what we argued about that last time?" he asked, bringing up the subject they'd been avoiding. The breakup that had led to the end.

Lissa's eyes filled with tears and she turned away. "I remember you being in a foul mood and I was just so tired of it. I knew school was hard for you, what with football practice and games, and you working at the gas station when you had free time. Still, we had a fight and agreed to take a break."

She wrapped her arms around herself and walked to the window. "Actually, I suggested the break, hoping you'd tell me I was crazy. Instead, you told me it was a good idea."

Trevor closed his eyes, remembering that argument clearly. As usual, her ex-boyfriend Bradley Banks had gotten under Trevor's skin. The captain of the football team and supposedly all-around good guy from the right side of the tracks, Banks was really a bastard beneath his moneyed looks. He'd always played on Trevor's insecurities, doing things like deliberately spilling a drink, then laughing and telling the rest of the team that Trevor's dad, who was the high school janitor, would clean up his mess.

"I'd bought you a necklace for your birthday." He vividly recalled the gold-plated heart with rhinestones around the edge.

"I still have it, tucked away in the back of a drawer," she admitted.

He'd wondered if she'd forgotten all about him over the years. Now he had his answer and his heart pounded harder in his chest.

Trevor looked over her shoulder and out the window, the glorious view a complete one-eighty from the small house he'd grown up in. The side of his house practically butted another home. When Trevor looked out his bedroom window, he could see the O'Reillys' back porch, so he'd had to keep his shades shut tight. Maybe that explained why he'd been drawn to this view, he realized now.

Lissa remained quiet, obviously waiting for him to continue. She stood alone, wearing his big shirt, as lovely and vulnerable as he'd ever seen her. But she still wasn't looking at him.

Well, this wasn't any easier for him, but it had to be done before they could ever move forward. If they could ever move forward.

"Do you remember what was bothering you that day?" she asked him.

He'd never told her.

He expelled a harsh breath. "Brad was giving me shit in the locker room, telling the guys I bought you a piece of junk at Sears and it was just a matter of time until you'd be sick of my poverty and back with him."

Though Lissa also lived on the "wrong" side of Serendipity, with her gorgeous face and luscious body, Brad had always seen her first as a prize, then as a challenge.

She turned around, eyes wide and angry. "That son of a bitch. Why didn't you tell me?"

He rolled his stiff shoulders, managing a shrug. "Because it was the same song, different refrain. The guy was a broken record and I have to admit that after a while, it got to me."

The man Trevor was now knew how stupid he'd been, but back then, he'd been humiliated and overwhelmed. "I guess I just needed to get away from the pressure for a little while." He stepped up beside her and pulled her into his arms. "I never meant I needed to get away from you, but I let it happen." She tipped her head back, leaning against his chest. "I figured out what an ass I'd been and tried to call you all weekend."

"But I didn't take your calls because I'd already…"

Her voice trailed off, both of them knowing the end of that sentence.

"Melissa Mayhue's parents were away and she had a party. I was upset and Brad and his friends were there. He passed me drinks and I took them. Can't blame him for that," she said, too much self-hatred in her voice. "And when I went to get my things to go home, he offered to drive me."

He stiffened, drawing on everything in him not to get angry and pull away so he could smash something and pretend it was her ex. The bastard had preyed on her vulnerability and taken advantage of her being upset that night. Then she'd gotten pregnant. Neither of them had been old enough or mature enough to understand it back then. It was still hard enough to accept now.

As much as he wished things had played out differently, he couldn't change the past. And it drove him crazy knowing that though Trevor thought Banks had done the right thing, in reality he'd merely given the Banks family the best public face while privately making Lissa as miserable as possible.

"I'm sorry," she said in a broken voice.

"I know you are." He turned her around, forcing her to look at him. "And so am I, sweetheart. So am I."

She sniffed. "Really?"

He nodded. "We share the blame for what happened. Hell, I realize now I bear most of it. If I hadn't agreed to split up, you'd never have been with him." Trevor knew that now as well as he knew his own name.

Her eyes shone with surprise and gratitude. "Thank you for that," she said, yet she moved out of his embrace.

In front of his eyes, she mentally and emotionally pulled herself together, internalizing the emotions she'd allowed to surface. "I'm glad we finally talked about this. I'm glad we had... closure."

Trevor blinked in shock at her stark words and suddenly cool tone. He'd thought he needed closure, too. No longer. Yet somehow she'd decided they'd wrapped things up between them in a nice bow.

But as far as he was concerned, things were even messier now than they'd been before. Because Trevor knew what meaningless sex was like—and what he and Lissa shared was a hell of a lot more. No way was he willing to let her just walk out of his life as if last night meant nothing.

"I don't know where you got the idea that last night was about closure," he said, folding his arms across his chest as he faced her down. "News flash, sweetheart. We're not close to over."

Lissa blew out a long breath and stared at him as if

he'd gone mad. "So... what? We're going to be together for another twenty-four hours, torture ourselves with what could have been... and then what? I'll go back to Serendipity, to my daughter—to Brad's daughter," she said bluntly. "And you'll stay here. Why prolong the agony?"

He couldn't deny she had a point. When it came to obstacles, they had plenty. Nor could he say he was ready to deal with everything her real life had to offer, including her daughter, her ex, and Serendipity.

"I don't have all the answers," he told her honestly. "The only thing I do know is that if it's going to hurt that much to walk away, it means there's something meaningful there to begin with." He held out his hands and waited, holding his breath.

"Damn it, Trevor," she muttered, and walked into his waiting arms.

He held her close and suddenly her stomach growled. He heard as well as felt the vibration and laughed.

"I'm hungry," she said.

"Let's go out and get breakfast."

She stepped back and gestured to his see-through shirt and her bare legs. "I have this and a formal gown," she reminded him.

"Personally, I like this."

She wrinkled her nose at him and he laughed. "Fine. Go shower. I'll give you a heavier shirt and a pair of sweats and socks to go back to the hotel in. You can change and then we'll go for breakfast. Better?"

She nodded. "Thanks."

A few minutes later, she'd shut herself in his bathroom and turned on the shower, while he lowered himself onto his bed and groaned, running a hand through his already messed-up hair.

He meant what he'd said a few minutes earlier. He didn't have any real answers for the future, but he'd just bought himself twenty-four hours with Lissa.

For now, that was enough.

FIVE

Still stunned by their heart-to-heart and the fact that Trevor wasn't letting her just leave, Lissa found herself sitting across from him at a small crepe place he said he enjoyed. She ordered an apple cinnamon crepe and they ate in a silence that was oddly companionable, considering the safe world she lived in had crumbled around her. She was facing interminable heartache and yet here she was, sitting across from him anyway.

"So what are your immediate job plans?" he asked.

She patted her mouth with the napkin and met his gaze. "Well, after I interview you, I have to go home and get to work on Ethan Barron. Do you remember him?"

He nodded. "My sister told me he came back to town after ten years, bought the Harrington estate, married Faith Harrington, and surprised the hell out of everyone in town by being a millionaire."

"After his parents died and he disappeared, everyone thought he'd end up in jail... or worse."

"Helluva story for you to write, though," Trevor said. "Then what?"

Lissa shrugged. "So far it's been freelance. I'm hoping something permanent will come up, but even this way I'm making more money than I was at Cuppa Café and writing the town obits." She lifted her coffee cup and took a long sip.

"Which means you aren't committed to staying in Serendipity because of your work?" he asked.

Her hands began to shake and she grasped her coffee cup for something to hold on to. "Serendipity is my home," she said, hoarsely. It was her security. "My family is there. My friends..." Hard-earned friends, she might have added. Because Lissa didn't let people in easily. In fact, she was better at driving them away. "Livvy's life is there."

Trevor shot her a knowing look, one that said he knew she was panicking. "Who are your friends these days?" he asked, smoothly changing the subject.

She didn't know why, but she was grateful not to have to think beyond right now. "You're really interested?"

Again, that knowing yet patient look crossed his face. "How else can I get to know you again?" he asked.

She sighed and shook her head, unable to deny him even the simplest of answers, even if he wouldn't like what he learned about her. "For awhile, I was lucky I had friends," she admitted. "I was unhappy, Trevor. Around Livvy I put up a good front, but when I wasn't? I was a raving bitch to most people." She couldn't meet his gaze, not proud of the woman she'd become for a while.

"Unhappiness can drain you."

He sounded like he understood, but she still couldn't look at him. "I'm lucky Kate Andrews decided she liked me. She'd come into the coffee shop, buy herself something, and hang out at the counter, talking to me when it was quiet and I wasn't serving."

"Kate…" he said as if trying to place her.

"Long, reddish-brown hair, best friends with Faith Harrington," she said, to jog his memories of their high school days.

He nodded. "I remember her. She was always outgoing. Nice."

"And persistent," Lissa said, wrinkling her nose at the memory. "She insisted I leave Livvy with my mom and come to Joe's with her and her friends on Wednesday nights. It's still Ladies Night. Soon Wednesdays became a ritual, and so did book club once a month. We rotate houses." She shrugged. "After spending most of my time holed up in the house, eventually I had friends again." She smiled at the thought of her small clique. "There's Kate and some other girls from high school, Stacy Garner and Tanya Santos." And now she even considered Faith Harrington one, too.

"And then Faith came back and your career took off…" he said, as if reading her mind.

Lissa shook her head. "It wasn't quite that simple." Drawing a deep breath, she recounted to Trevor how godawful rude she'd been to Faith on her return to Serendipity.

"When Faith got together with Ethan, I took great pleasure in reminding her that though he could wrap a woman around his finger, he didn't know the first thing about sticking around." She winced at the reminder, knowing she'd said far worse to Faith—and God, she regretted it.

"Are you trying to scare me off?" Trevor asked, reaching across the table and grasping her hand.

His heat seared her skin but the warmth in his eyes undid her, crumbling defenses she'd tried so hard to build. "I just want you to know who I am, so there are no surprises."

He grinned. "You're forgetting I've seen you at your worst. I also know you only act out when you're feeling jealous or threatened."

Lissa's cheeks flushed with embarrassment. "Yeah, well, maybe I was jealous. From the outside, it seemed like Faith had it all. Even with her father in jail, she came back and opened a business, immediately fell back in with her old friends... and things were so difficult for me at the time..." She trailed off, thinking about Faith's story. "I didn't know how hard it had been for her until the interview. Not that anything excuses my behavior." In fact, she'd punish her daughter if she ever treated anyone the way Lissa had Faith.

"Maybe you were afraid that since Faith had returned, she'd take Kate away from you and you'd really be alone?"

Trevor's perceptiveness took her off guard.

She was mortified he'd homed in on the one thing she'd never admitted out loud—or even to herself. Faith's return home had threatened the life she'd built, but how had Trevor known? It was so scary, how well he got her, and yet he wasn't running away as fast as he could.

She didn't understand it. Her life never went the way she wanted and so she couldn't begin to trust this fragile thing they were building. Yet Trevor was persistent—with his words, his understanding, and his gentle touch. Even now, he maintained contact, his thumb rubbing circles over her wrist.

"I'm guessing that didn't happen?" he asked gently. "Kate stuck around?"

Lissa managed a smile along with a nod. "Of

course Kate ripped into me for how I treated Faith and she was right, too. But Kate's persistent. She just kept including me and including Faith. We even did karaoke together at Joe's."

Trevor grinned. "I'd have paid good money to see that."

Lissa grimaced. "Not something I want to repeat."

His expression sobered as he said, "But Faith gave you that interview when she could have called on any well-known reporter who'd have killed for her story. There must have been a reason."

Lissa shook her head, still dumbfounded by that. "To this day I don't know why, but I'll be forever grateful that she did. Faith taught me about humility and forgiveness and so many other things."

Trevor treated her to a warm smile. "That's what I admire about you—your willingness to admit when you're wrong. Sometimes it takes a while and you come around kicking and screaming, but you do it and that takes guts." He cleared his throat. "So does having a baby at eighteen and living through a hellish marriage."

Lissa blinked in surprise, a lump forming in her throat. "Don't go canonizing me. I'm still no saint," she reminded him.

"Especially not in the bedroom," he said, his eyes darkening. And that quickly, serious conversation was over.

*   *   *

Lissa and Trevor parted ways after breakfast. Trevor decided to head into the office to get some work done while Lissa went to her hotel room to begin working on the article about him. In truth, Lissa suspected he needed time alone as much as she did.

Time to remind herself that despite how easily they fit together when they were alone, life wasn't about living in a bubble and they had way too many obstacles between them to think about a future. Back in her hotel, she settled in with her laptop and began writing about Trevor Dane. The boy who'd pulled himself up and out of Serendipity to become one hell of a man.

By the time the evening approached, Lissa had accomplished more than she'd hoped for considering her state of mind, and she'd even managed to take a nap. She luxuriated in a warm bubble bath and then pulled out the simple black dress Trevor's secretary had chosen for the dinner party.

From the things Trevor had said and things her research had indicated, Alexander Wittman was a big part of Trevor's life, his mentor as well as his friend. For that reason, Lissa wanted to make a good impression—and not just as a reporter doing a story. Though it was silly, if Trevor was going to bring her as his date, she wanted him to feel proud. Last night had been easier. Dressed in a ballgown and feeling like a princess, she'd almost been able to believe she belonged at the event.

But now, as Trevor helped her out of the limousine, nerves assailed her. Though he hadn't taken his hungry gaze off her, and though he clearly approved of the way she looked, her insecurities came rushing back. After all, if her husband, the man whose baby she'd borne and who'd married her, hadn't seen her as country club material, why would Trevor's business associates and friends see her any differently?

When she'd attended as Trevor's reporter/date, she had been able to put those feelings aside, but now that he was looking at her possessively, she was petrified she'd fall short and embarrass him.

Unaware of her inner turmoil, he placed a hand at the small of her back. "Ready?" he asked.

She let out a deep breath. "Of course." She walked toward the waiting doorman, who opened the door for them.

"Good evening, Mr. Dane. Mr. and Mrs. Wittman are expecting you," he said, nodding politely to Lissa and acknowledging her with a smile.

"Thank you, George. See you on our way out." Trevor steered Lissa away from the bank of double elevators and toward a separate single lift down the hall. "This way," he said.

Once they were alone outside the small elevator,

Trevor turned to her. "What's wrong?"

She shook her head and forced a smile. "Nothing. Why?"

"You're uptight and your spine's so rigid I'm afraid it'll break," he said, grasping both her hands in his. "Are you nervous about meeting Emma? Don't be. You'll love her."

Lissa shook her head, feeling stupid, but if she didn't let out her fears, she'd definitely screw things up even worse. "I don't belong here," she said on a rush.

"What?"

"The private elevator, a dinner party where we're dressed nicer than any dinner I've ever been to…" She shook her head and swallowed over the lump in her throat. "If you were bringing me here as the reporter to cover your story it would be one thing, but—"

He squeezed her hands tighter, forcing her to meet his gaze. "But what?"

Just say it, a small voice in her head insisted. "But my own husband didn't want to be seen with me at formal events. These people you love so much are going to take one look at me and know I'm so far out of my league—" She cut herself off, horrified by the truth she'd blurted out.

She'd meant to be honest. Just not that honest.

An angry muscle twitched in Trevor's jaw.

"I didn't mean to upset you." She was making a

mess of a night that meant a lot to him.

"You didn't upset me. That asshole you married did." Trevor took a minute to breathe and let go of the rage simmering inside him.

No matter how opulent the apartment, he and Lissa came from the same world. He'd had the same insecurities, probably more so as he'd had to navigate alone. She had him by her side.

"I'm sorry Brad made you feel inadequate in any way. You are spectacular and the people upstairs will know it the second they lay eyes on you. Because they're real and nothing like the Bankses of the world." Speech finished, Trevor cupped his hand around her cheek and pulled her in for a kiss.

One light enough not to ruin the makeup she'd obviously spent so much time applying, but one sincere enough to make his point. "Do you believe me?" he asked.

Eyes wide, she merely nodded.

He hoped she meant it because he sure as hell had. "Ready?" he asked her.

"Ready," she said, her voice hoarse.

Trevor nodded. "Good."

The night went better than Trevor could have hoped. Alex and Emma clearly liked Lissa and made her feel at home, as did their small group of guests. By the time ten o'clock rolled around, Trevor was ready to get her out of there and be alone with her, when Alex waylaid him.

Together they walked to a private corner. "She's something special," Alex said.

Trevor inclined his head. "That much I know."

"But? I sensed tension from her earlier tonight."

Trevor nodded. Alex had always been perceptive. It was why he'd done so well in business. He was good at reading people. "She doesn't think she belongs here," he said, frowning at the notion.

Alex raised an eyebrow. "Did anyone say something to make her think that?" he asked angrily.

"No. It goes back a long time," Trevor said, not wanting to divulge Lissa's personal insecurities. "She thinks we live in different worlds now."

"I see." Alex nodded knowingly. "She does have a valid point."

Narrowing his gaze, Trevor glared at his friend. "What exactly does that mean?"

"Breathe, boy." Alex laughed and gestured toward a passing waiter to bring them each a drink. "Serendipity isn't exactly Manhattan. Can you blame her for feeling a little out of place? I'm sure she'll adjust in time."

"Only if she wants to."

"You both have to want to," Alex said.

Before Trevor could respond, the waiter returned

with two glasses on his tray. "Scotch on the rocks," he said.

Trevor accepted a glass, as did Alex. "Thank you." The waiter nodded and walked away.

"They're hitting it off," Alex said, his gaze drifting toward the corner of the room where Emma had pulled Lissa away for a private chat.

Trevor was grateful the other woman was making an effort at helping Lissa feel more comfortable, but he didn't plan on leaving her alone for too long.

As always, Alex's gaze softened as he looked at his wife. The man, a shark in the boardroom, was a marshmallow at home. "Relationships are a two-way street, you know."

"I'm trying," Trevor said. Hell, he was doing his damndest to convince her they could make a go of it. "It's only been two days…" His voice trailed off, knowing time didn't mean a damned thing. They'd known each other for too long.

"But there are ten years to get over," Alex said. "Not to mention a lot's happened in that time. You've been a confirmed bachelor, while she's a mother."

As always, the reminder felt like a physical punch in Trevor's gut. "I know."

"Do you?" Alex asked, putting a hand on Trevor's shoulder in a fatherly gesture.

"What are you saying?" Trevor asked.

"Just this. Before you ask her for anything, make sure you can handle her life and everything that comes with it. It's not fair of you to ask her to let you into her life unless you're sure you want all of her, including her child."

His stomach cramped and he suddenly felt the weight of responsibility he hadn't thought of before. "We haven't discussed it," Trevor said.

"And you haven't given it much thought because you've spent the weekend in bed," Alex said, guessing correctly.

Trevor broke into a sweat. He wasn't sure whether to thank Alex for making him face the truth, or to deck him for bringing it up.

"One thing is for sure—no matter how you come by them, children are a lifetime responsibility and when they're stepchildren, so are their biological parents," Alex said. "Now, I know I've given you a lot to think about. Let's go join the women."

With a new weight on his shoulders, Trevor followed Alex over to Lissa, suddenly panicked, knowing he couldn't possibly jump into the idea of being her daughter's father overnight.

Alex was right. Either Trevor was all in or he bailed before either of them got hurt.

And deep down, he feared it was too late for that.

*　　*　　*

Trevor was silent on the way home. Too silent, and Lissa couldn't help but fear his thoughts. For the last two days, she'd been telling herself this weekend was all they had—but inside, she couldn't deny there was a flicker of hope. She wanted more, and he'd done his best to indicate that he did, too.

But ever since he'd returned from talking to Alex earlier, Trevor had been more withdrawn. "Would you mind if we went back to my hotel room?" she asked, knowing that even if they spent tonight together, it would be easier on her if he left in the morning. That way she could just fall apart instead of having to be the one to walk away.

"Sure." He sat by her side in the town car, but unlike their last few rides, he kept his hands to himself.

Another bad sign.

She fingered her small bag, her nerves getting the best of her until finally the driver pulled to a stop in front of the hotel. A doorman immediately stepped up and opened the car door, then stood back and waited.

Lissa exhaled a long breath and turned to face him. "Thank you for taking me with you tonight. It was a pleasure to spend time with Alex and Emma, since they both mean so much to you."

The evening had also filled out her article in im-measurable ways, but she wasn't in the mood to bring up business.

He smiled at that. "When I was younger, they helped me feel welcome, Alex in business and Emma on the social side."

She nodded in understanding, then reached for his hand. "Trev, I'm so glad we had this time together." It was more than she'd ever dreamed of and less than she wished for deep inside.

"Does this mean you're not inviting me up?" he asked, his voice gruff.

She swallowed hard. "I wasn't sure you'd want to come."

His blue eyes darkened. "I probably shouldn't, but I'm selfish enough to want more. I want tonight," he said, his voice hoarse.

Oh, he was definitely preparing for the end, she thought. A far cry from the man who'd faced her earlier. But she wasn't ready to ask questions she didn't want the answers to yet. So, though she knew she'd hate herself for prolonging things, she met his gaze and nodded.

"I want that, too." She slid out of the car before she could change her mind, and held out a hand, indicating he should come, too.

The next few hours were the most beautiful and the most painful of Lissa's life. Trevor held her hand as they made their way upstairs to her hotel room and locked the door behind them.

He undressed her slowly, taking his time because they had all night. What they didn't have was a lifetime, and that was the only thing that would satisfy the yearning inside her. Still, she wanted these last moments and she made sure to recall each and every one. His strong, tanned hands gliding over her skin, his dark hair as he bent over her, his mouth taking her breast and suckling and teasing, torturing her until her need was so great, she thought she'd come from that alone.

He worked his way down her body, making love to her with his tongue, worshipping her in the way only a man could, replacing memories of them at seventeen with those of a night stolen out of time. One that belonged to them alone.

And by the time he lifted his body over hers, poised for entry, she'd already come more times than she could count, yet she still hadn't had enough of him. She never would.

With his gaze fused to hers, he nudged at her opening and slowly eased his way inside, making sure she felt every last inch, every ridge, every thick hard part of him. Only when he thrust home, so deep she knew he was touching more parts of her than he'd ever reached before, did he lose control.

"Lissa." Her name a groan, he pulled out and thrust back in, her own moisture creating a slick haven for him to pound in and out of her, bringing her up higher and higher.

She tried her best to hold back her emotions, to take the ride and just feel everything inside her and process later, but the tidal wave of feelings he created was too great.

"Trevor." His name came out on a sob, triggering his release.

He didn't hold back either, murmuring words of love and caring, words she absorbed into her heart and her soul, sensing this was the last time she'd hear them out loud.

And as he took over her body, coming inside her, he carried her up and over with him. Stars exploded around her, inside her, shattering her heart in the process.

When their breathing slowed and he pulled out, separating their bodies, he curled himself around her and held her tight. Neither said a word, Lissa holding back sobs but letting the tears fall. And later still, when hours passed, he'd made love to her one more time before she fell into a fitful sleep.

Lissa awoke to the feel of him sliding away from her and out of bed just as the sun began to creep through the window.

She knew her options. She'd weighed them each time she woke in his arms during the night—remain silent, pretend to be asleep, and avoid a painful goodbye; or get up and fight for what she wanted.

She'd spent yesterday telling herself it was better for them to separate now, but the more she thought about it, the more she had to ask herself why. Fate had brought them back together at a time when they had no obstacles in their way, unless they put them there. This time there was no pregnancy and no other man.

True, Lissa had a child, but why couldn't Trevor get to know Livvy and accept her as Lissa's little girl, and eventually as his own? Many men accepted other men's children. Even with their intertwined past, they should be able to do this.

She owed it to herself to at least reach for what she wanted. Heart pounding, Lissa pulled herself to a sitting position in bed, lifting the sheet to cover her naked body. "Trev?" she asked softly.

He turned. The only light in the room came from the sun filtering through the drapery. "I didn't mean to wake you," he said.

"Were you going to just slip out without saying goodbye?" She brushed her tangled hair off her face.

"I would've left a note." He sounded as sheepish as he ought to feel, Lissa thought.

"Don't go yet." She patted the space beside her, but he remained standing and shook his head.

"I thought... I think we should make this as easy on ourselves as possible."

She raised her eyebrows. "Says the man who insisted this wasn't closure? That if it hurt, it meant there was still something between us?" she asked, throwing his own words back in his face. "I admit I'm the one who was ready to throw us away, but I was wrong. What changed on your end?" she asked, hating how her voice trembled. But she had to know what happened.

"I thought about what you said yesterday. About the things that separated us. And I thought about something Alex said."

Uh-oh. Lissa's heart began to thud against her chest in a painful beat. "And what was that?"

Trevor reached for his slacks, pulling them on before speaking. "He brought up more things than just the distance between New York and Serendipity and the disparity in our lifestyles. He said I shouldn't push you for anything until I was sure I could accept everything your life involves."

And in that moment, Lissa knew exactly what Alex had said. "You aren't sure you could accept Brad's child as your own," she said dully, the pain hurting so much more than she could have planned for.

He spread his hands in front of him, as he so obviously searched for the words to explain. "It's more than that. It's whether I'm ready to be a father. To be honest, I gave up that dream when I lost you. I dove into college, work, and making a life for myself."

Lissa nodded slowly, digesting his words, believing part, dismissing the rest. "Let's be clear, okay? This has nothing to do with whether or not you want to be a father. Whether you can adjust your bachelor life. This is about me having Brad's baby and you having to face that every time you look at my daughter."

Her jerked as if she'd struck him, but to his credit, he pulled himself together.

He rolled his shoulders back and met her gaze. "I don't know. Maybe that is it. But could you blame me?" he asked, his voice rising. "Could you really blame me for having a tough time with it?" He sucked in a breath, then muttered a low curse. "Shit. I didn't mean it that way."

He sure as hell had, Lissa thought. She closed her eyes and only when she was sure she could speak calmly did she look him dead in the eye. "Not only did you mean it, but I have an answer to your question. Yeah, I sure as hell *can* blame you. Not before yesterday, but after. After you looked me in the eye and told me we weren't over. Now this?" She shook her head, devastated beyond words. "Just go," she said, wanting to him to leave so she could be alone when she cried.

She turned her head and waited. She felt him standing there staring at her and she held her breath, wondering if he'd crawl onto the bed, pull her into his arms, and say he'd made a mistake.

Instead, she heard him dressing and getting himself together. After an interminably long time, the hotel door shut behind him, leaving Lissa alone.

She turned and rolled into the pillow that smelled like him and sobbed for what felt like hours before dragging herself out of bed and into the shower.

She had a daughter she adored and a life to get back to. There was no way she could go home with swollen eyes so her perceptive little girl would ask her why mommy had been crying.

*   *   *

Trevor waited until he was alone in the elevator and slammed his hand into the metal wall, grateful for the pain throbbing in his knuckles. Better to focus on that than the pain searing his heart.

He hadn't walked out on Lissa easily or lightly, but he'd done it based on the main thing Alex had said that made sense. *Before you ask her for anything, make sure you can handle her life and everything that comes with it.*

Was Trevor sure he could handle dealing with Brad Banks as Lissa's ex-husband, as her daughter's father? Could he be a stepfather to a little girl who probably adored a man Trevor hated?

He didn't know, but he'd better figure it out soon—before he lost Lissa for good.

SIX

It was amazing what one could accomplish with a broken heart, Lissa thought, not for the first time since her return from New York. When she'd finally pulled herself together and showered, she'd found a note slipped under her door in Trevor's handwriting. "I'll always love you."

At the time, she'd thought it was a sweet but pointless gesture and she'd tucked the paper into her bag, one last memory of the weekend. Now, two weeks had gone by. Life had gone on. Lissa had baked cookies for Livvy's bake sale at school, she'd helped her daughter with her homework, and she'd argued with Brad about canceling his next weekend with Livvy. He'd promised he would take his fiancée to Cancun and wanted Lissa to break the news to their daughter. When Brad refused to change his plans, she informed her ex-husband he could damn well disappoint his daughter himself. Lissa wasn't doing his dirty work for him.

In the meantime, the *News Journal* had been so

happy with her article on Trevor, they'd made a permanent job offer. Thanks to the beauty of computers and the Internet, she could work from anywhere, and she'd eagerly accepted. The magazine had gone to print on Trevor and was on newsstands now. She'd made sure to overnight a copy to Trevor, but she hadn't signed a note of her own.

She'd interviewed Ethan Barron and discovered just how hard his life had been, how much he'd had to overcome, and how he'd done it all on his own. He'd returned to his hometown to face the wrath of the brothers he'd left behind and fix his life. Along the way he'd discovered a teenage half-sister he didn't know he had, and both he and Faith were raising her together. No, it wasn't easy, but being together with the woman he loved made it simpler.

That's when Lissa lost her "star-crossed lovers" point of view and got angry at Trevor for not being willing to try.

Her doorbell rang and Lissa opened it. She'd been expecting Kate to come by.

"Ready for the game?" Lissa asked, referring to the annual homecoming football game between Serendipity High School and their crosstown rival.

Kate nodded. "You?"

"No. But I'm going anyway." Lissa wasn't in the mood for big crowds and people, but she knew she was better off getting out of the house.

"Where's the munchkin?" Kate, the schoolteacher who loved kids, looked over Lissa's shoulder, looking for Livvy.

"Olivia Rose, let's go!" Lissa called out.

Livvy came bouncing down the hall in the Serendipity colors, maroon and white, with a streak of white on her nose. "Aunt Kate!" she called happily when she caught sight of her favorite nonrelated grownup.

"Hey!" Kate pulled her into a hug. "What's that you've got on your nose?"

"Mommy put face paint on!"

"She's in the spirit," Lissa said by way of explanation.

"At least one of you is," Kate said, her serious gaze on Lissa.

"Go get your coat. It's a little chilly out," Lissa said to her daughter. She waited until Livvy was out of earshot. "I'm fine."

"You look pissed off," Kate said, too observant as usual.

"I'm just hurting," she admitted. "I'll get over it."

Kate tugged her into a hug. "I'm sorry. I wish things had worked out for you and Trevor. He has no idea what he's missing."

Lissa managed a smile just as her daughter bounded back into the room, coat in hand. "Can we go now?

Can we? Can we?"

"You're right. He doesn't." She gave her daughter a loving look. "Everyone ready for the game?" Lissa asked brightly, smiling for Livvy's sake. No need to dull her enthusiasm.

They piled into Kate's car and soon found themselves at the high school for the big game. As usual, whenever Lissa came by the school, memories assaulted her, some good, some bad. Today was a true mix loaded with might-have-beens.

But unlike in years past, when Lissa would wonder what would happen if she and Trevor met up again, this year she knew. All that was left now was to come to terms with it and put him behind her once and for all.

*   *   *

Trevor hadn't been to the Serendipity High School football game since his senior year. And he wouldn't be here now except that he was on a mission. Two weeks ago he'd walked out on the woman he'd always loved and he hadn't had a good moment since. What he had had was time—time to regret, time to mourn, and time to think.

He regretted how he'd handled things that last morning. He'd let Alex's talk of children being forever and Livvy being Brad's daughter put him into panic mode. He should have taken a deep breath and talked things through with Lissa. No doubt that's what Alex had intended with his father/son-like talk. Instead, his words had sent Trevor running.

He'd mourned the years they'd lost and used the time to think about whether he was going to let old insecurities hold him back from the future he'd always wanted. Brad Banks had managed to destroy Trevor's past, but if he lost Lissa again, Trevor would only have himself to blame for his future.

When he'd decided to make a spur-of-the-moment trip to Serendipity, he'd planned on heading directly to Lissa's. But his sister had informed him that today was the annual homecoming football game and Trevor knew everyone in town would be there, Lissa included.

Well, if he wanted to make a statement, this football game was the place to do it. How Lissa reacted would determine the rest of his life, and Trevor's stomach was in knots the entire ride home. He hoped she'd be relieved to see him, but then again, after he'd walked out on her he figured he'd have more of a challenge on his hands. No matter what, his weekend with her and then his time alone had convinced him she was worth it.

They were worth it.

He arrived at the field and immediately saw his old friend, Nick Mancini. Grateful for a familiar face,

Trevor called out to him.

"Hey, buddy. How have you been?" Trevor slapped the other man on the back.

"I'm hanging in there," Nick said. "Keeping busy despite the lull in new construction. How about you? I saw the article Lissa wrote on you. So you're still making it on Wall Street?" Nick grinned in approval.

Trevor nodded, not wanting to discuss the article or the messengered copy he'd received from Lissa, no personal note included. If that wasn't a kick in the gut, he didn't know what was.

"Yeah. I got lucky myself," he said to Nick. "Somehow I rode out the massive wave of firings a couple of years ago and my company bounced back big."

The two men turned toward the field. Trevor braced his arms on the fence and watched the play. "Looks like the team's got a chance this year," he said.

When Nick didn't reply, Trevor turned and realized the other man wasn't paying attention. Instead, Nick was focused on two women and a little girl in the distance.

Lissa and her daughter. Trevor's mouth went dry at the sight of them and an auburn-haired woman who he thought was Kate Andrews.

Nick couldn't tear his gaze away from them and Trevor narrowed his gaze. "What's got you so distracted?" he asked, accenting his question with a shove to get his attention.

"Women," Nick muttered.

"Which one?" Trevor asked, not needing Nick interested in Lissa on top of everything else.

"This you won't believe."

"Try me," Trevor said.

Nick groaned. "Kate Andrews."

Trevor released the breath he'd been holding.

"The woman is going to be the death of me," Nick said, unaware of Trevor's thoughts.

"You? And Kate?" Lissa hadn't mentioned Kate seeing anyone.

"Is it that odd?"

Trevor shook his head. "I thought you went for blonds."

Nick shrugged. "It took me by surprise, too, but after Faith and I agreed we were in the past—"

"You picked up with Faith Harrington again?" Trevor remembered Nick and Faith being a couple back in high school and her breaking up with him.

Nick shook his head. "Never had another shot with her with Ethan Barron in the picture. But the truth is, Faith and I are just friends. Whatever chemistry we had is in the past." He glanced over at the women once more. "But Kate thinks she's my rebound girl while I'm getting over Faith."

"Is she?" Trevor asked.

"Hell, no."

Nick frowned, looking like a man truly in distress, and Trevor couldn't help but take pity on him. "So why are you standing here with me when the woman you're interested in is over there?"

When the woman Trevor wanted more than his next breath stood with her.

"Good question," Nick said, and before Trevor could blink, Nick headed off in the women's direction, calling out Kate's name.

Both of them turned and Lissa's gaze locked squarely on Trevor, her shock evident. Following Nick, he headed over, hoping that having Kate around would ease the conversation at least until he could get her alone.

He glanced at the little girl jumping up and down beside them and talking to her mother and Kate, and reassessed. *If* he could get Lissa alone.

"Ladies," Nick said first, tipping his head in acknowledgment. "You're looking good today, Kate."

"Funny, Mancini." Kate smirked, her moss-green eyes, darker than Lissa's, narrowing in distrust.

"That hurts, Kate." Nick placed a hand over his heart. "See what I mean?" He turned to Trevor. "She doesn't take me seriously."

"Any reason why I should?" Kate asked.

Nick straightened his shoulders, meeting her gaze. "Because I'm me. And I never say what I don't mean."

Trevor had known Nick for years and he'd never heard him more serious.

But Kate merely rolled her eyes.

Lissa shook her head and Trevor tried not to laugh. The poor guy obviously had his work cut out for him if he wanted to get Kate to believe in him.

"Hi, Lissa," Nick said, turning his attention away from Kate.

"Hi, Nick," she said, obviously aware of Trevor right beside him.

"Hi, Lissa," he said, his voice gruff.

"Trevor." She treated him to a tight smile.

Kate glared at him, obviously well versed on their recent past.

"Who's this beautiful girl?" Trevor bent down so he was eye level with Lissa's daughter, well aware this was his one and only first chance. He got this right or he went down in flames.

As he looked into green eyes so like her mother's, Trevor nearly lost his breath. "I bet you're Olivia," Trevor said, putting his hand out to her.

Laughing, she put her smaller hand inside his for a grownup shake. "My friends call me Livvy."

"Well, hi, Livvy. My friends call me Trevor. I'm an old friend of your mom's."

She tipped her head to one side and looked him over, obviously judging him. He actually held his breath, while Lissa, who'd moved closer to her daughter, did exactly the same thing.

"Does that mean I can call you Trevor, too?" she asked, looking up at her mother.

Lissa clenched her jaw, obviously torn and not knowing how to answer.

"Livvy, want hot chocolate?" Kate asked, holding out a hand.

"Yes! Mommy, can I get hot chocolate with Aunt Kate? Please, please, please?" Being Trevor's friend was forgotten in favor of a special treat.

Trevor straightened.

"Sure, baby. Go on," she said, giving her daughter's hair a ruffle before sending her with Kate.

"Let's go, Nick." Kate shot a command at the man.

"Drinks on me, ladies." Nick, clearly clueless about the underlying dynamics between Lissa and Trevor, was just happy to be included and headed off with Kate and Livvy.

"She's going to make him work for it," Lissa said, watching the trio until they disappeared into the crowd.

Trevor shrugged. "Seems to me he's more than willing to do whatever he needs to in order to make her believe in him." He met Lissa's gaze, hoping she understood he was talking about himself as well.

"Lucky her." Lissa shoved her hands into her oversized sweatshirt.

She'd worn her long hair pulled back into a ponytail, with very little makeup, and she looked, in a word, tired. As though she hadn't been sleeping well, either, Trevor thought.

"Lissa—"

"Trevor, look, we're bound to run into each other from time to time—which is weird since ten years passed and we managed to avoid each other—but that's life. If you could do me a favor and stay away from Livvy, I'd appreciate it. She doesn't need mixed messages in her life."

"I couldn't agree more."

"Good. Thank you."

"Don't thank me just yet. I agree she doesn't need mixed messages. But my message isn't mixed. Not anymore."

Lissa's expression went from neutral bordering on stiff to clearly nervous. She looked around, noticing the people passing by, catching sight of them, some whispering, some pointing.

Serendipity was a small town, population approximately 2,500, and yet it seemed like everyone knew everyone else. In this case, the fact that Trevor and

Lissa were breathing the same air was news. Just as he'd known it would be.

And clearly she was just now realizing it, too. "We can't talk in front of all these people," she said on a sharp whisper.

"Yes, we can. Because what I have to say can damn well be said in front of an audience." He hadn't planned things this way, but now he realized it was his one shot at making her believe in him.

In them.

"I screwed up."

Her cheeks flushed pink. She folded her arms across her chest and raised an eyebrow, but she stood still. She was listening.

"I shouldn't have walked away two weeks ago. I thought about you and me and the past... and I panicked."

"And now you're fine? Now you can handle the fact that the daughter I love more than life itself is also Brad Banks's daughter? How does that work, exactly?" she asked, staring him down even as tears streamed down her face.

He reached out and took her hands. They were shaking.

"It works because I say it does. Because I lost you once for ten long years. And because instead of talking to you about my fears, I left you a second time—and

I'll be damned if I'm that stupid again." Trevor's entire life flashed in front of his eyes as he laid out his feelings for Lissa—and at this point, half of Serendipity—to hear.

She pulled one hand back and ran her sleeve over her damp eyes. "Damn it," she muttered. "You as much as agreed you couldn't look at my daughter and not see a constant reminder of what went wrong." Her other hand shook inside his.

"I was an idiot. When I looked into that little girl's eyes I saw you and only you."

"Brad gets Livvy every other weekend," Lissa said, her voice trembling. "And when he shows up, he comes to the door, I let him into the house, and he picks her up. We're civil for our daughter's sake."

Trevor saw exactly where she was going with this. "I can do that, too. I'm just wondering if it can be done from Manhattan instead of from here. Of course, Serendipity is only an hour from the city, so if you insist on staying, I can also adjust to the commute."

"I got a job with the *News Journal*," Lissa said, addressing the only thing that seemed real to her at the moment. "They're located in Manhattan."

Trevor's grin held both excitement and pride. "We'll talk," he assured her, obviously not making snap decisions for her.

She still wasn't sure she could take it all in. She

supposed that was due to the fact that she wasn't sure she could hear correctly with all the noise. Her vision was blurred with tears, and she just hadn't expected him here. As for his sudden turnaround... could a girl get that lucky?

"Sweetheart, I said I can be civil to your ex. As long as we don't have to invite him for holiday dinners." Trevor cocked an eyebrow.

Yet she still didn't understand and until she did, she couldn't accept. "You walked out on me in New York." She addressed the thing that kept her up at night and threatened to choke her during the day.

He held her hands in front of him and squeezed her tight. "I'm sorry I let you go without a fight the first time. I'm sorry I didn't step up and offer to marry you despite you being pregnant with his child. And I'm really sorry I walked out in New York. But I'm not going to lose you again."

Lissa's throat was full, her heart was pounding so hard she could hear it over the crowds, and she was still scared she'd wake up and discover this was all a dream. After all, the last ten years had been a lonely nightmare. "Trevor—"

"Wait. There's one more thing I want to say before you speak, okay?"

She managed a nod, grateful for a few seconds to pull her thoughts together.

He reached into his pocket and then suddenly went down on one knee. "Elisabetta Gardelli, will you marry me? I'll wait as long as you want, spend all the time in the world getting to know and love your beautiful daughter and proving myself to you, but in the meantime… will you wear this ring? And promise you'll marry me eventually?" he asked with the most endearing grin on his handsome face.

But his expression was more serious than she'd ever seen it, and his hands weren't steady as he knelt before her and the entire town of Serendipity, ring in hand.

And what a ring it was. Though blurred by her tears, Lissa knew that sucker was huge. But she didn't care about the size or the shape or anything more than this man proclaiming his love for her and promising to love her and her daughter.

"Till death do us part, Lissa. What do you say?"

"Yes! Yes." The words had barely passed her lips when he grabbed her and swung her around in his arms.

"You'll never regret it, sweetheart. I'll make you happy every damned day for the rest of my life."

Lissa wiped her happy tears as he put her down long enough to slip the ring over her finger.

Suddenly she noticed her daughter standing beside Trevor, looking at him with wide, curious eyes. He bent so they were eye level. "What is it, pretty girl?" he asked.

Her look was a combination of wariness and child-like curiosity. "Now do I get to call you Trevor?" she asked.

Lissa grinned and nodded.

And the crowd around them erupted in applause that had nothing to do with the score of the game.

Lissa wasn't sure she deserved such happiness, but she was definitely going to enjoy each and every minute. After all, it wasn't every day a girl got a second chance with the only man she'd ever loved.

Other Carly Classics

The Right Choice

Suddenly Love (formerly titled Kismet)

Perfect Partners

Unexpected Chances (formerly titled Midnight Angel)

Keep up with Carly and her upcoming books:

Website:
www.carlyphillips.com

Sign up for Carly's Newsletter:
www.carlyphillips.com/newsletter-sign-up

Carly on Facebook:
www.facebook.com/CarlyPhillipsFanPage

Carly on Twitter:
www.twitter.com/carlyphillips

CARLY'S MONTHLY CONTEST!

Visit: www.carlyphillips.com/newsletter-sign-up/ and enter for a chance to win a $25 gift card! You'll also automatically be added to her newsletter list so you can keep up on the newest releases!

If you enjoy books on the steamier side, don't miss my "Dare To Love" series. Read on for an excerpt of Dare to Submit…

Dare to Submit
Excerpt

ONE

She submitted without the comfort he'd expect to see from a woman who'd been coming to this club for over six months. In the main room, members were in all states of dress, some naked, some in leather, all comfortable with themselves. She dropped gracefully to her knees, legs spread wide, palms up, and yet he sensed her discomfort from across the darkened room. The sound of pleasure, of sex, of pain echoed from the play areas nearby. To most, it was familiar, comforting. It should be the same for her, but her posture was too stiff, her entire demeanor, too wary. Possibly because she played with a different man each time. Searching for something. For what? Decklan Dare wondered, not that he understood why he cared. But she called to him. Had from the first.

So he watched her. Just as he watched for her arrival, uneasy when too much time passed between her visits. She didn't show up more than once, sometimes twice a month. He wasn't here much more often but tried to time his visits with what he knew of her past schedule. Ridiculous. She was just another female and not one he'd ever played with, at that. But she was soft and rounded in just the right places, curvy in a way that appealed to him when no one before had ever reached that deep.

He shook his head and told himself to move on. Find someone else. Someone who knew he had no expectations but for the night. But he no longer used the club for pleasure. He'd tired of it awhile back. He came to relax here with friends, that's all.

His gaze fell back to *her*. She shifted her body uncomfortably and Decklan frowned. He'd always disliked protocol. He'd never expected it. Didn't need it. He'd bet she didn't either. She just needed a man she believed in, that was apparent.

Not him. She looked too vulnerable for someone who took, gave the minimum, and walked away.

"Still fighting it?" his best friend, Max Savage, asked.

Decklan cocked an eyebrow. "Fighting what?" he asked although it was stupid to play dumb. Max knew him better than he knew himself.

"Yourself. Go play with her. Get it out of your system." Max eased himself onto a barstool beside Decklan. "Better than watching her and wondering. Besides, you need to get laid."

Decklan clenched his fist in his hand. His brother,

Gabe, had told him the same thing. "You know as well as I do I can't give her what she needs."

Max barked out a laugh. "Like you'd even know what that is?"

"I can guess. Does she look like she's found the right guy? She comes here and tries out different men. Obviously she's not into exhibition, because she ends up in one of the private rooms for whatever her kink happens to be, he gets her off, and the next time, she's on to the next guy."

"Sounds perfect for someone who doesn't do relationships," Max said, gesturing to the bartender for his regular scotch on the rocks.

The club had a one-drink maximum. Alcohol and consensual play didn't go well together. Decklan had already had his, ordered it the minute *she'd* walked in. One look at her curves, the full breasts, perfect indentation at her waist, and that luscious ass he'd like to squeeze, and only a drink would do.

"Or maybe she hasn't found what she needs and she's looking for a relationship of some kind," Decklan said, guessing at what the beautiful woman was really in search of.

He didn't do those. Had thought neither of the Dare brothers did those. He'd been wrong. Gabe had found Isabelle, and now Deck was left wondering if there was something wrong with him.

Max ran a hand through his longer blond hair. "You could always walk away after."

That was the problem. Decklan was afraid one night with her wouldn't be enough.

He scowled at the scene across the room. She still wasn't comfortable, and Mike, her chosen man of the night, wasn't a patient dom. The monitors had had to intervene more than once in a scene he'd performed, and Decklan watched the duo warily. Maybe that was what she sensed, what made her unable to find her peace.

But in position, her long blonde hair fell over her back. And Decklan's groin tightened at the sight. Every cell in his body rebelled at the notion of the other man's hands on her body, or worse, him thrusting into her wet heat. No doubt that would be the end result. Why else would she choose a private room for play?

"Let Mike fuck her tonight." The bastard now tangled his hands in her hair.

"She doesn't always sleep with the guys she plays with." Max sounded pleased as he imparted the information, then took a long swig of his drink.

"How would you know?" Decklan asked, his shoulders stiffening even more.

The other man shrugged. "I negotiated a scene with her once."

An unexpected wave of jealousy turned Decklan's vision a blurry haze, and he grabbed Max's shirt, only to have the man laugh in his face. "It was before you'd laid eyes on her."

Feeling ridiculous, Decklan released his friend.

"And she wasn't interested in having sex with me." Max smoothed out his shirt, his grin still annoying the shit out of Decklan. "Does that change things for you? Maybe she's not looking for anything but subspace and a couple of orgasms. Surely you can handle giving her that?"

"Fuck you, man."

"Sorry. You're not my type." Max laughed.

Decklan closed his eyes, wondering if the lack of sex with her partners did make a difference. If she just came here to scene and relax, that he could handle. Maybe. But if she wasn't sleeping with someone until she'd established a deeper level of trust, that was beyond his ability to give. But he didn't know how much longer he could go on like this, watching, unable to get her out of his head.

The sound of raised voices caused his eyes to snap open.

Mike stood and she'd risen to her feet. Her full breasts nearly spilled over the leather corset binding her body with enticing hooks Decklan wanted to open one by one.

Mike said something.

She shook her head.

The dom's face grew hard and he grabbed her hair.

Her eyes opened wide. "Red." She said the word loud and clear.

Instead of releasing her, Mike yanked her hair harder.

In less than a heartbeat, with Max right behind him, Decklan was out of his chair and heading across the room. He wasn't about to allow a woman to be taken advantage of in his presence. Especially not *this* woman.

*   *   *

"Come on, let me be the first one in this club to get into that pussy." Mike, the dom Amanda had agreed to scene with tonight, pulled her hair harder than she liked, especially when she wasn't near to being aroused by him.

"No." She cringed at the thought. Hadn't they already negotiated? Laid down the accepted rules and boundaries? She'd been uncomfortable all night, and now she knew why her instincts had been on high alert.

"No?" This time he yanked on her hair to show his displeasure. "What about me and my friend?" He spoke louder than was appropriate or necessary, and she blushed as people around them began to look. "One of us in that tight pussy, another in your ass?"

Hell no. "Red!"

"Get your hands off her." This from the man whose dark gaze followed her everywhere but whom she'd never met.

"What's going on here?" John, a club monitor, approached. Fully dressed in leathers and wearing a badge indicating his status, his arrival was exactly what Amanda needed.

He turned a hard and pissed gaze on Mike, the man she'd stupidly opted to play with tonight.

He stepped into her personal space, getting between her and Mike, the asshole. Apparently he had a protective streak.

"The lady said red. Mike didn't respect it. You can take care of the bastard. I've got *her.*"

John nodded, pulling an argumentative Mike away for what looked like a good dressing down.

"Thank you," Amanda said to her rescuer, admiring his take-charge personality, which turned her on as much as his good looks already did. She'd had her eye on him for months.

Cropped, jet-black hair and a strong, chiseled face that knocked her on her ass. He had an air of authority that aroused her.

"My pleasure." He smiled, taking her breath away.

Until now, she'd only seen him from across the room. His impact was more potent up close.

She only came to the club once in awhile, to try and get what she needed from a guy without the hassle of a relationship. It still amazed her she'd only ever really desired *him*. But he'd never approached her, and she wasn't the kind of woman to take what she wanted from a man. Never had been. Didn't trust the reaction she'd get in return. There was a reason she had a membership here, where expectations were laid out up front and if someone approached her, he wanted her, if only for the night.

He clearly hadn't.

The deeply ingrained insecurities instilled by her perfection-demanding mother rose to the surface. Too fat. Not pretty enough. Passably smart, but where would that get her?

"Let me take you out of here," he said in a gruff voice, pulling her back to the present. She met his gaze.

The unexpected flare of desire in his dark blue eyes took her off guard. If he'd approached her earlier or another time, she would have taken him up on the invitation. Now, it seemed like he'd made it because he felt sorry for her. She'd been someone's pity fuck once before. Never again. Insecurities were one thing. Being stupid quite another.

"Thank you but I'm fine."

"No, you're not." He lifted her trembling hand, which made his point for him.

He obviously thought she was upset about the incident with Mike. He was wrong. She was overwhelmed by his masculine scent, and her body trembled with the effort it took not to take him up on the offer. Pheromones didn't care about things like emotions and pity fucks.

"I don't know you," she said, throwing out another, more substantial roadblock.

Even he would understand that after the crap Mike had pulled, not even the security of club membership assured her anyone here was safe. He couldn't expect her to leave with him.

As much as she wanted to.

She shivered, suddenly cold, wishing she were wearing day wear and not this stupid corset and short leather skirt.

"I can vouch for him," Max Savage said. He was a nice guy she'd done a scene with awhile back. He'd relaxed her and taken her close to subspace. Not over. No one took her there. And at the time she'd been with Max, she'd had no interest in sleeping with him.

This guy was another story.

She glanced at Max and tried not to grin. One friend trying to help another get laid. "Nice try, but I don't know you all that well either."

She rubbed her hands up and down the goose bumps on her bare arms.

"What if I told you he was a cop?" Max asked.

"Really?"

He extended his arm, and someone handed him a blanket, which he proceeded to wrap around her shoulders.

"Thank you," she said, immediately feeling better.

"You know me." John, the club monitor who'd hauled Mike away, reappeared by her side. "You can trust Decklan to take care of you. Mike's been warned before. His membership has been revoked."

She blinked in surprise. "I'm glad." The asshole didn't deserve to be in a position of trust.

"Decklan's a decent guy. Don't leave with him if you don't want to, but at least let him get you something cold to drink. You'll feel better, and then you can get changed and leave. I'll walk you out myself," John promised.

Decklan. She tested the name in her head, liking the sound. "A soda sounds good."

The crowd around them had already dispersed, and even Max had walked away, giving his friend a shot on his own.

Good luck, she silently told him. To her way of thinking, they might have passed *I'm interested* looks with their eyes over the last six months, but he hadn't stepped up, which Amanda took personally. Decklan whatever-his-last-name-was would have to bring his A game if he expected her to do any more than drink a soda with him before heading home.

Carly Phillips

About the Author

N.Y. Times and *USA Today* Bestselling Author Carly Phillips has written over 40 sexy contemporary romance novels. After a successful 15 year career with various New York publishing houses, Carly made the leap to Indie author, with the goal of giving her readers more books at a faster pace at a better price. Carly lives in Purchase, NY with her family, two nearly adult daughters and two crazy dogs who star on her Facebook Fan Page and website. She's a writer, a knitter of sorts, a wife, and a mom. In addition, she's a Twitter and Internet junkie and is always around to interact with her readers.

CARLY'S BOOKLIST
by Series

Below are links to my series on my website
where you will find buy links for each novel!

Dare to Love Series

(www.carlyphillips.com/category/books/?series=dare-to-love)

Dare to Love

Dare to Desire

Dare to Surrender

Dare to Submit

Dare to Touch (coming January 2015)

Look for more Dare to Love series books in 2015!

Other Carly Classics

The Right Choice

Suddenly Love (formerly titled Kismet)

Perfect Partners

Unexpected Chances (formerly titled Midnight Angel)

Carly's Earlier Traditionally Published Books

Serendipity Series
(www.carlyphillips.com/category/books/?series=serendipity-series)

Serendipity

Destiny

Karma

Serendipity's Finest Series
(www.carlyphillips.com/category/books/?series=serendipitys-finest)

Perfect Fit

Perfect Fling

Perfect Together

Serendipity Novellas
(www.carlyphillips.com/category/books/?series=serendipity-novellas)

Fated

Hot Summer Nights (Perfect Stranger)

Bachelor Blog Series
(www.carlyphillips.com/category/books/?series=bachelor-blog-series)

Kiss Me If You Can

Love Me If You Dare

Lucky Series
(www.carlyphillips.com/category/books/?series=lucky-series)

Lucky Charm

Lucky Streak

Lucky Break

Ty and Hunter Series

(www.carlyphillips.com/category/books/?series=ty-hunter-series)

Cross My Heart

Sealed with a Kiss

Hot Zone Series

(www.carlyphillips.com/category/books/?series=hot-zone-series)

Hot Stuff

Hot Number

Hot Item

Hot Property

Costas Sisters Series

(www.carlyphillips.com/category/books/?series=costas-sisters-series)

Summer Lovin'

Under the Boardwalk

Chandler Brothers Series

(www.carlyphillips.com/category/books/?series=chandler-brothers-series)

The Bachelor

The Playboy

The Heartbreaker

Stand Alone Titles

(www.carlyphillips.com/category/books/?series=other-books)

Brazen

Seduce Me

Secret Fantasy

Made in the USA
Lexington, KY
13 July 2015